The Fragrance of Surrender

Souls of the Sea: Book 1

A novel

APRIL GEREMIA

Psalms96:3 Press

Books by April Geremia

The Fragrance of Surrender
(Souls of the Sea Book 1)

The Leap of Forgiveness
(Souls of the Sea Book 2)

CONTENTS

Prologue 1
Chapter 1 2
Chapter 2 12
Chapter 3 17
Chapter 4 26
Chapter 5 37
Chapter 6 43
Chapter 7 49
Chapter 8 57
Chapter 9 67
Chapter 10 79
Chapter 11 87
Chapter 12 100
Chapter 13 111
Part Two: One Week Later...119
Chapter 14 121
Chapter 15 138
Chapter 16 144
Chapter 17 159
Chapter 18 170
Chapter 19 184
Epilogue 188
About the Author 189

DEDICATION

For my family—those who have left to be with our Lord, those who remain nearby, and those whose lives have taken them far away. I love you all, and can't imagine my life without you.

Prologue

Gabriella only half understood what she was about to do. After all, she wasn't a believer. She couldn't have understood that the Host of Heaven stood by, silently urging her to utter the prayer that would put into motion the plan that was set before the beginning of time. There was no way for her to fathom what it meant to trust her child's life to God and His plan. She couldn't anticipate the gnawing pain of uncertainty, the painful releasing of her own will, the unimaginable loosening of her embrace. The awful, relentless letting go.

No, the only thing on Gabriella's mind at that moment was the life of her only son. The punishing rain whipped hard against her skin, and she felt the urging of unseen forces. A determined gust of wind compelled her to her knees—the tears of soul-understanding violently coursed down her cheeks.

"God, if you're really there," she whispered. "Please don't take my son away from me."

Gabriella paused, tried to quell the panic threatening to overwhelm her. The wind continued to push her to the ground. She swallowed roughly and lifted her eyes toward the sky. She was desperate, would do anything if only Sammy could live. Even petition this God she had grown to hate. "If you'll spare my Sammy, I promise to relinquish control of his future and put it into your hands. I make this oath to you: Let him live, and I'll give him back to you."

And so it was.

Chapter 1

Three Months Earlier

Gabriella stood as close to the edge of the cliff as possible without toppling over the 300 foot drop, then looked down at the jagged edges cascading downwards until abruptly dropping into the rolling blue-green sea.

She inhaled, steadied herself, and raised her eyes toward the heavens and all of its seemingly unreachable mysteries. Then she raised her arms toward the sky, fists clenched tightly, and exhaled. It was in these moments—when she dared the sea, the world, even almighty God Himself—to swallow her whole, that she felt most alive. Only here, one tiny step away from death, did she feel life stirring within her.

It hadn't always been this way.

Five years ago, Gabriella had been happy. She'd been married to Nicolas, was the mother of a young son who was the light of their lives, and lived a comfortable lifestyle that had left her feeling, if not completely satisfied, then as close to it as someone could possibly expect in this life.

Gabriella met Nicolas the year after she graduated from college. She was the adopted daughter of her poor immigrant aunt—he the cherished son of an elderly couple who'd been blessed with fertility later in life. They were a study in contrasts, these two, the laid back all-American boy and the fiery Latin immigrant. He was charming with his offbeat features: solid build, blonde curly hair most men his age had already outgrown, and soft green eyes that lulled you into an unexpected comfortableness. Gabriella was tiny with exquisitely delicate features set off by a wall of blue-black hair cascading down to the small of her back. Her face wasn't beautiful, not even pretty, but it had a bottomless quality to it that made people want to push in and find out who she was.

The following years were filled with freshly baked apple pies and tamales, sweet sixteen birthday parties and quinceñeras, bobbing for apples and smashing piñatas with brightly wrapped broom handles. It was a multicultural family life marked by love and warmth and an easiness few people are lucky enough to enjoy.

But that was over three years ago, before she and her son moved to Rendiciòn, a tiny village located on a remote island in Latin America that time had seemingly left behind. Now everything was different, and on more days than she cared to admit, she found herself dangling on the edge of the cliff, trying to find a reason why she shouldn't let herself fall over it. She gazed into the endless expanse of blue-green, and felt the familiar longing pushing up against her insides, demanding to be heard. Gabriella wanted so much to be there again, back in time to the place before things had gone so terribly wrong. But she couldn't go back, would never again be in the place where she lived in ignorance of just how cruel life could be.

That choice, of whether to live or die, to allow herself to fall over the cliff, or to stand still and try to make sense of a life gone so wrong, gave her something solid to hold on to. It put the decision about what would happen next in her hands, instead of leaving it to chance. And because she hadn't been in control of her life for so long, the idea of deciding for herself was intoxicating. But Sammy, her ten-year-old son complicated things.

The easy way out would be to fall into the nothingness she so craved, but she would never do that to Sammy. He needed her, still loved her, despite the fact that she'd been emotionally absent for so long. And she of all people understood the importance of family to a child.

Before she married Nicholas, Gabriella hadn't been part of a family, not truly, not in the way she'd always longed for. Abruptly abandoned by her parents at an early age, she'd been left to maneuver her way through life with her only guide a stressed out and emotionally unavailable aunt who said she had no choice but to take in her sister's kid. After all, she was the only family left, her aunt had grudgingly muttered year after agonizing year.

And so throughout Gabriella's life, she'd clung to the few early memories she had of her parents. Those of life in the pale yellow house on the cliff. When her life had been light and not dark, filled with laughter and not tears, love and not abandonment.

And now, as she allowed the memories to come, she tasted the salty sea air the winds drove inland, heard the clamoring of the waves, felt the sting of the sea spray carelessly spit out by the roguish waters. She remembered what it was like to be enfolded in warmth, a love that knew no boundaries, a sense of security that all was right in the world. This is the place in time she wished had stood still—that place of belonging, of not desperately wanting or needing.

But it hadn't.

Those memories, those elusive fragments from her past, were from before her parents mysteriously disappeared into the night, never to return. It would be easier, she often thought, if she could just forget those happy times because they left a gaping hole in her already torn-apart heart. This not knowing, this wondering why her parents would walk away and leave her behind had always been a force to contend with for Gabriella. It grew up with her, becoming bigger and taller and wider right alongside her, like a shadow bully who followed her relentlessly wherever she went.

Her aunt had been mute on the subject, even as she laid dying with Gabriella at her side pleading with her not to take the secret to her grave. But she slipped away anyway, tightly clutching to the knowledge that would have set free a portion of Gabriella's heart.

Which is why she clung so fiercely to Nicholas and his parents. When she married him, she not only gained a husband, but a loving family as well.

They saw her for who she was—someone once loved and accepted. Nicolas' parents somehow sensed she carried memories from the past just outside herself, too frightened to truly claim them as her own. So they embraced her in a way that made it impossible to refuse. Slowly, steadily, she allowed herself to be taken into another family, and soon found herself immersed so deeply she forgot to allow for the end—that inevitable moment in time when everything you live for and love comes to an abrupt halt.

It came on an impossibly wet morning, one of driving rain, low smothering clouds and frantically moving windshield wipers. When the policemen came to the door in their black, dripping slickers to deliver the news that Nicolas' parents were dead—that they'd never even seen the truck barreling down the wrong side of the slick highway, she immediately chastised herself for falling for the illusion. It always ends this way, she told herself. With a *leaving*.

But instead of letting go of those she loved, distancing herself to avoid the inevitable pain, she held on tighter, trying desperately to change what destiny surely held.

Now, a sympathetic breeze swirled around the cliff and disturbed the hem of her peasant skirt, and Gabriella realized she was holding her breath. It was always this despair, this hopelessness of her life that brought her to the edge of the cliff, but it was the thought of that next step, that plunge into utter darkness that drove her back to life. Here, so close to eternity, she could barely discern the faint whispers in the wind telling her there was more.

But what?

She desperately wanted—needed—to know where she would land if she allowed herself to fall. Into the hands of the so-called loving God as Nicolas had tried to tell her, or into an all-consuming black abyss?

Ah, yes. Nicolas.

She shut her eyes against the sun's glare and tried not to feel. The loss was still too fresh, too sharp to bear. A mere ten years ago, she and Nicolas had shared the unspeakable joy that stems from watching the child of your love push his way into the world. Sammy had come out screaming, a scrapper, a forceful personality from the start. He'd delighted, mystified and worried his parents with his colorful antics, his wide-open heart and his unquenchable curiosity.

As Sammy grew, he and Nicholas, who were father and son lookalikes, became inseparable. Both were light, fair-skinned and freckled with unruly blonde curls toppling over their foreheads. Nicolas was a sturdy man, he had the kind of build that hints at honor and dignity and old-fashioned values. Sammy inherited Nicolas' build, as well as his eyes—green and soft, reminiscent of the moss that comfortably settles in the soft spot of a pond.

Gabriella loved to watch her little boy mimic Nicolas. If he wore a red shirt, Sammy would quickly change into a matching one. If Nicolas put his hand against a doorframe and leaned into it, Sammy would be right there, copying his movements precisely. It was an easy few years, the kind of time that pleasantly melts away like the last of the butter on a warm kitchen counter. So she tucked away her fears of misfortune, her ever-present sense of doom, and despite the pledges she made to herself never to be lulled into a false sense of security again, she failed to steel herself against the calamity waiting just outside the door. And so it snuck up on her. Insidiously. Deceitfully. Cruelly.

On the cliff, Gabriella inhaled the heavy salt air, and began to think about the night when their world was irreversibly shattered.

It began when Nicolas was invited to a men's retreat in South Texas by one of his co-workers. He decided to go because the man was one of his supervisors and he didn't want to offend him.

"Who knows, mi amor? You might have fun," teased Gabriella.

Nicolas sighed. "I just wish the timing was better. I'm so exhausted I think I could sleep for days."

She lowered her head, letting her long tresses hide her concern. While it was true that Nicolas was putting in long hours at work, it couldn't possibly account for the level of exhaustion he'd felt for the past few months. She'd begged him to see a doctor, but he believed if he could only catch up on his sleep, he'd be fine. But he was sleeping away most weekends and seemed to be getting more and more tired. "Nicolas," she began…

He dropped a stack of shirts into his open suitcase and came to her, gently taking her small face in his hands. "I know what you're going to say, and you're right. I'll make an appointment with the doctor first thing in the morning."

She smiled, relieved. "Thank you. I'm sure it's nothing, but it will make me feel better, okay?"

He pulled her close to him and spoke softly into her ear. "Don't worry, Gabby. I'm sure everything is fine."

She nodded, battling back the familiar sense of unease.

A noise by the door interrupted them, and they turned in unison to find Sammy struggling with his child-sized suitcase.

"Daddy? I'm all packed. When are we leaving?"

Nicolas and Gabriella looked at each other, trying to discern in each other's eyes where the misunderstanding had occurred. Nicolas knelt down beside Sammy. "I'm afraid I'll have to go by myself this time, son."

"Huh?" Sammy said, dropping his Spiderman suitcase with a thud. He pushed back the mop of curls falling over his forehead. "I thought you said it was a men's treat."

"Well..."

"So, I'm a man. Why can't I go?"

As Gabriella watched the scene, she noticed Sammy had once again emulated Nicolas' clothing—this time they wore blue jeans and a yellow pullover shirt. Nicolas put his hands on Sammy's shoulders, which shook with the indignation of being left behind. "Son, sometimes a man has to think of others before himself. Now, if we both went, who would be here to take care of your mom?"

"We could get a babysitter."

Nicolas smiled and shook his head. "She doesn't need a babysitter. She needs a man in the house. You'll have to be that man while I'm away."

Gabriella watched Sammy process the information. He went from being on the verge of tears to standing up straighter, a new determined look on his face. "I'll do it, daddy! I'll be the man of the house while you're gone."

Nicolas had hugged him. "I knew you wouldn't let me down, son. I'm counting on you."

The sun went behind a cloud and the change in light distracted Gabriella. She sighed, felt herself sway a bit, pushed by a malevolent wind from the north. The memories were enough to make her consider slipping over the edge of the cliff, but then images of Sammy came to her mind. Her little boy had been through so much, and she wouldn't cause him any more pain. But the ache she felt in her heart was unrelenting, and she didn't think she could continue with it as her constant companion.

She let the memories take her back again. She had been shocked when Nicolas walked in the door after the retreat. He looked exhausted, and it appeared as if he'd aged in the short time he was away. But she couldn't look away from his eyes. They looked like they had all the light in the world stored in them.

"Nicolas!" she cried, rushing toward him.

He didn't refuse her offer to carry his suitcase, and when he sank deep into the sofa, he closed his eyes to steady himself for a moment. When he opened them, the light was still there.

She struggled to focus on his words because she was so concerned about his health. It turned out the retreat had been a Christian one, and Nicolas was excited about the things he'd heard.

"I found Him, honey," he said with a quiet awe in his voice. "The one who can give us life that never ends."

"We need to get you to the hospital," she countered. "I've never seen you so sick."

"We've been living our lives for the wrong things," he said. "Things that will fade away instead of what's eternal."

She put her wrist against his forehead. "Amor, you're running a fever. When is your appointment with the doctor?"

"Oh Gabby," he sighed, sinking deeper into the sofa. "He loves us so much. I never knew. I just never knew."

"Vamanos," she said, irritation tinging the word. She stood up and tugged on his arm, but she wasn't strong enough to move him. "Let's get you in bed, and I'll call the doctor myself first thing in the morning."

Nicolas reluctantly and with great effort pushed himself off the sofa.

"Gabby," he said, taking her by the shoulder and gently turning her toward him. "I just want you to know what I do. To see what I've discovered. It changes everything, honey."

She let out her breath, tried to remain patient. "Right now," she said. "All I want to see change is your health. Really, Nicolas, let's get you in bed before you fall down."

The salt air stung her eyes, and Gabriella momentarily freed herself from the memories. Nicolas died less than a year later from a particularly nasty and aggressive form of cancer.

So, he did leave after all.

"Some God you are," she hissed bitterly. She clenched her fists tighter and ignored the wind as it ruthlessly began to whip her hair against her face. Against her will, her thoughts turned to the time when her and Sammy's world was forever altered.

After Nicholas' death, Gabriella had slipped into a deep depression, a feeling of wanting to fade into the background, never to resurface again. Over the next couple of years, she retreated from her friends, stopped returning calls and began to forbid all references to God in their home. It angered her that Nicolas had put all his trust in this God who had abandoned him when he was sick.

She stopped doing things the way they had as a family. She didn't cook the same meals, keep the same schedule, and she got rid of the familiar things in the house and replaced them with functional, serviceable items. Otherwise, each meal was a reminder of what she'd lost, every familiar event caused her to experience the pain as if it were new. She couldn't bear to sit on the same sofa Nicolas had. Eat from the same plates. Sleep in the same bed.

She was a woman desperate to escape the pain, and in her mind, eradicating all the memories of Nicolas and their lives together seemed the only way to cope. But she knew it was wrong. Nicolas was the love of her life, and the hero of Sammy's world. Yet, no matter how much her mind told her she needed to keep things normal and familiar for Sammy, her heart couldn't find a way to do it. The guilt that followed crushed her. She was robbing Sammy of his chance to grieve, she knew, and he wouldn't be able to heal naturally from the loss. Her heart screamed at her to do what was right for Sammy, and yet no matter how hard she tried, she couldn't. Nicolas' death had destroyed her. It had turned her into a woman whose actions were solely driven by her pain, and although she saw the damage it was causing, she couldn't find a way to stop.

The further she retreated from their old life, the more prominent one thing became in her mind: The yellow house on the cliff where she had spent those precious few years with her parents. When she first felt called to the waterlogged, forsaken seaside village perched high on a cliff, she tried to ignore it. After all, why try so carefully to tuck her life behind her only to go in search of another faraway painful past?

But she longed to go there again. Her father had spent his childhood years roaming those hills and helping with the small orange grove that supported the family. Then her parents inherited the place when they married, just as she had when her aunt died.

Thinking about the old house made her nostalgic, longing for what she'd lost so long ago. She remembered baking in the kitchen all day with her mother as a child, and then losing herself for hours in the orange grove as she played in her imaginary world. The memories were gauzy and drifting, but left her with a sense of pleasantness and comfort. The urge to return to the house had become so strong, so persistent, she'd finally given in to it just to give herself some peace.

So she'd packed up her and Sammy's life in Texas and left everything and everyone behind to travel to this left behind part of the world in an attempt to contain the damage. Life is too unpredictable, she decided, too out of control. So she meticulously and deliberately reduced their once expansive life into a smaller, more manageable one. Smaller is safer, she reassured herself. Less of a chance for the unthinkable to happen. Surely death and disaster wouldn't follow them to the ends of the earth.

But no matter how far she ran, she couldn't hide from the fear, the anger and the sense of being betrayed by everything that called itself good.

And so instead of the longed for peace, more days than not she found herself dangling on the edge of the cliff, listening intently to the elusive voices in the wind for some explanation of why things had gone so horribly wrong.

Now, she closed her eyes and rallied her fists again against the sky. "Where are you, great and terrible God of Nicolas?" she screamed toward the surging sea. "And why have you made me your enemy?"

Chapter 2

Sammy stepped off the age-weary school bus and was met by the thing he hated most in the entire world—an empty house. Again. He glanced nervously toward the cliff, shrugged his backpack from his lanky arms and flung it onto the front porch. He headed down the dirt path that led to the orange grove, scuffing his green Keds and the hem of his blue jeans along the way.

School was finally out for the summer—a fact that immensely satisfied him. He and his mom moved here three years ago when he was halfway through the second grade, and although he hadn't been too excited about it at first, he'd learned to appreciate life in the yellow house. But things in the house weren't the same as they were in Rendición, the village at the base of the mountain. While at home, he felt comfortable—as long as his mom was in a good mood, but the village always felt tense, ripe with disagreements about the way things should be. The odd mix of old and new created a constant source of battles in the community: crusty old fishermen with cell phones and their resentful wives who still did their laundry in large wooden tubs behind their houses. The younger villager's refusal to wear plaids and stripes together alongside the older folk's derision about their vanity. Modern, brightly painted road signs that would mysteriously disappear overnight, only to resurface the next day as an exotically colorful bonfire surrounded by the old men cheering at yet another hindrance to progress.

At times, it seemed as if the fiercely differing desires of the masses would boil over and erupt, but so far the townspeople had managed to keep it buried under the surface. But it was there, Sammy sensed it every time he went to town. Underneath the villager's forced smiles and handshakes festered the outward pushing of the old against the new. Of progress verses sameness.

And the smells. While at first repugnant, they'd grown on Sammy. The smell of the too-small fish rotting in the sun after being caught and later discarded mingled with the fragrant scent of ripening oranges that clung to everything in the village.

But mostly, Sammy stayed at home. He liked the slow pace that made him feel as if he could breathe for the first time since his dad died. It would be the perfect life if his mom hadn't gone off the deep end.

Sammy entered the grove, found his lucky tree and began his daily search for the perfect orange. He felt each orange along the branches as he did every day after school. This one's not ripe enough, the color's a little off on this one, bugs are on this one, and then… ah yes, he spotted the perfect one. Sammy carefully plucked it and slid down the trunk to the ground beneath the orange laden branches. Poking his thumbnail into the top of the fruit, he peeled away the soft skin. He'd picked a good one—juice slid down his chin as he bit into the orange. Chewing contently, he sighed deeply.

Summer was here, and he had a monumental task ahead of him.

A few weeks ago, he began to hear the rumors about the cliff. At first he didn't believe it—his mom would never do anything so dumb. But one day he saw it for himself. The school bus had taken a detour that day because a hard rain had washed away the regular road.

It had looked as if she were flying. Her arms stretched upwards, and she was so close to the edge he couldn't see the ground underneath her feet. As the school bus rolled by that gray and misty day, everything seemed to move in painstakingly slow motion. Sammy had looked out the smudged window in helpless terror as his mother seemed to decide whether she would live or die. It was in that moment his summer mission came into focus: He'd learn about the God his father tried to tell him about before he died. Maybe then he'd understand how life could be so messed up.

But there was a problem. His mom didn't allow him to talk about God, so he couldn't ask any questions about Him. But something inside of Sammy urged him to pursue this elusive God. Partly because of the way his dad had been so peaceful even as he laid dying in his bed, but also because the ache inside him for something good and happy and pure was so strong that he would do just about anything to satisfy it. That, and the fact that his dad seemed so sure.

"Sammy," his dad had said, pushing away the soup he delivered to him moments earlier. He hadn't eaten in days. "There's more to life than this, son. When I die, I'm going to Heaven to be with God."

"Can I come with you?" Sammy asked quickly.

His dad shook his head. "It's not your time, yet. But if you put your trust in God, I'll meet you there one day."

Sammy tried to pay attention to his words, but had trouble concentrating. His dad, so strong only months before, was now so skinny and kept having to catch his breath between sentences. Sammy wanted to pull him out of bed and take him to the backyard for a game of catch. But instead, he stared at the bluish-black half-moons under his eyes and tried to make sense of things. He felt afraid. Like something really bad was happening that he couldn't stop.

"Do only men go to Heaven?"

His dad grinned and then winced with pain. "No son, everyone who knows Jesus gets to go."

"Uh-huh." Sammy looked down. He didn't think it was fair that his dad was moving to Heaven without them, and they wouldn't be able to go with him until they met this Jesus person. He started to protest, but when he looked up, his dad's eyes were closed. Maybe he'd fallen asleep again.

Sammy waited for some time to speak, but his dad's eyes stayed shut. Finally, he couldn't stand it any longer. "Well..." he said impatiently. "Where is he?"

"What?" his dad asked groggily.

"Jesus. Where is he?"

His dad kept his eyes closed, but managed to move his once strong hand over his. "He's everywhere, son. All you have to do is seek him and God promises that you'll find Him."

Well, it hadn't been that easy. Sammy started in the living room, turning over every pillow and looking behind and underneath every chair, sofa and table in the room. Next, he searched the kitchen, dining room, bathrooms and the bedrooms one by one. Then, he went outside to the backyard, tripping over his and his dad's baseball mitts making him that much more surly. He looked in every inch of the yard, including the tool shed which was strictly off-limits. After a long time of searching, Sammy felt frustrated.

He huffed back to his dad's room to tell him that this Jesus person may be everywhere, but he was definitely not in their house.

In his haste, he didn't notice the chaos until he stood in the middle of it. Strangers rushed around in the bedroom, all wearing the same blue shirts with badges on the front, and they all looked very serious. A big cart with wheels stood in the middle of his parent's room, but he didn't know what sat on top of it because a white sheet covered it. Only then did he notice—his daddy was gone.

Sammy stood still while the people in blue whispered to his mom, who sat on the bed right where his dad had been the last time he saw him.

"Mom?"

No one heard him, or at least no one paid any attention to him.

"Mom?" he said again, his voice cracking with the effort. "Where's daddy?"

This got a few looks from the people in blue, but when he searched their eyes, they quickly looked away. Two of the strangers pushed the cart with the white sheet past him in a hurry.

His mom didn't move, but sat on the bed staring at the cart as it went through the door.

"Mom?"

This time she looked at him, but didn't seem to know who he was. He took a step closer. "It's me, mom. Sammy. What's wrong?"

"Your father," she whispered.

The only remaining man in the room stepped toward his mom, spoke in soft tones that Sammy couldn't hear and handed her something. He walked toward the door and when he was halfway there, he turned around went back to Sammy. The man rumpled his hair affectionately and silently walked out of the room.

Sammy reached up and smoothed out his hair, never taking his eyes off his mom. He went to sit beside her. He didn't say anything, and neither did she but the clock on the wall made all sorts of noise.

Sammy looked at the bedside table. "He forgot his watch."

"What?"

"Daddy forgot his watch. See? It's right here."

His mom finally drew him in close with a sob. "He's gone, Sammy. Your father's gone."

"Where did he go? Did he already move to Heaven?"

She sat there so long that Sammy thought maybe she hadn't heard him. Then finally, "Yes, Sammy. Your father's gone to Heaven."

The way she said the word made him think Heaven might not be such a nice place after all.

But that day on the bus as Sammy remembered his dad's words, he made a promise to him. He would look for Jesus again, and this time he'd find him so they could all be together again.

And as he had strained to see the fading figure of his mother on the cliff, he made another promise to his dad: He wouldn't leave her behind.

In the grove, Sammy crammed the last of the orange into his mouth, wiped his hands on his jeans, and then reached into his pocket to pull out a well-worn piece of paper. As he looked at it, he had the feeling it would change everything. Summer's here, he told himself. It's time to be the man of the house.

Chapter 3

By the time Sammy got back to the house, Gabriella was in the kitchen working on dinner. Sammy plopped down at the scarred wooden table.

"What's for dinner?"

"Well, hello to you, too."

"Sorry, mom. Hello. And what's for dinner?"

Gabriella shook her head, amused, as always, at the mischievous ways of her son. "Well, I thought we'd celebrate the end of school with your favorite meal."

"Pizza?"

Gabriella nodded. "Pizza."

"With ham and pineapples?"

"Is there any other kind?"

Sammy smiled his lopsided grin and pushed at an errant curl. "Thanks, mom. I'm pretty excited about summer vacation."

"You know, there will be a lot of work this summer in the grove. Raul hasn't been feeling well lately, and I'll be counting on you to help him."

Raul was the foreman who worked the grove, and his mom said he had also worked it when she lived here as a little girl. When they had first arrived, the trees in the grove were barely producing any oranges. His mom said the only reason they weren't dead was because Raul had taken care of the grove the entire time the house had been empty because he couldn't stand to see the trees die. But they had all worked hard for the past three years to reestablish it, and now, in their third year, they were finally going to reap a harvest.

To Sammy, Raul looked as old as dirt, and he didn't think he should be working anyway, but his mom said Raul needed the grove as much as it needed him. Anyway, he liked Raul and loved to listen to his stories about the old days.

"Don't worry," Sammy said. "I've watched Raul for long enough that I know what to do. Do I get to be the boss?"

She looked away and smiled. "No, Raul will still be in charge, but you'll be his right-hand man."

Sammy nodded, cautiously fingering the piece of paper in his pocket. His mom was in a good mood, and this might be the perfect time. In a moment of bravery, he pulled it out and smoothed it flat on the table.

The motion caught Gabriella's attention. "What's that?"

"Um… Well…"

She stopped kneading the dough and turned around. When she saw the handbill, she wiped her hands on the apron and moved toward the table.

Sammy quickly covered the sheet of paper with his hands.

She sat down. "What is it Sammy?"

"You have to promise not to get mad."

"Uh-oh," she said. "This already sounds like trouble."

"Mom, it's just that this is really important to me, but you're not going to approve."

"Okay…"

"But I'm almost a grown-up now…"

"You're ten."

"And I think it's time I made some decisions on my own."

Gabriella sighed. "Sammy, move your hand, and let me see what's under there."

Sammy slowly sat back, cautiously taking his hands off the paper.

Gabriella's face hardened, and she returned to the counter where she began pounding the dough. "You know my thoughts on the subject, son."

"Yes ma'am. But they don't match mine."

She stood still, then slowly turned around, a look of immovability on her face. "I'm sorry, Sammy, but this subject isn't open for discussion."

Sammy started to protest, but she held up her hand. "I understand you're curious about this God thing, but I've heard about these tent revivals. They get people all worked up with fake healings and made-up stories, and then they ask them for all of their money. I won't let you be taken advantage of."

"But mom. Dad—"

"—Dad was wrong."

Sammy stared, open-mouthed, at his mom. The statement hung heavily in the air. His dad was wrong? But he'd seemed so sure, so happy about what he'd learned about God. How could he have been wrong about something that had given him so much joy? He looked at his mom. Her face was so tight, so unbending, and he thought back to his dad's face before he died. He'd been so peaceful and content. He'd seemed so *sure*.

A tremor of realization spread though Sammy's body as he realized the shocking truth of the situation: his mom was the one who was wrong. His mom. Wrong.

"Do I make myself clear, Sammy?"

He closed his mouth and sat up straighter. "Yes, ma'am," he said as he folded the handbill and stuffed it back into his pocket. He felt awful about what he was planning to do. He'd never set out to deliberately disobey his mom before, but it was the only thing he could do. It was, after all, a promise he intended to keep.

The celebration dinner was tense and stilted and Sammy barely tasted the pizza anyway. His mom tried to make it up to him by talking about the summer and the fun things they could do, but Sammy knew it was just that—talk. They hadn't done anything fun since his dad died.

"What about spending the entire day at the beach looking for seashells?"

"Sure, mom."

"Or maybe we could pack a lunch and picnic by the cliffs."

"The cliffs?"

Gabriella quickly looked away.

"Look mom. It's okay—you don't have to entertain me anymore. I'm ten now, remember?"

She attempted a smile. "Yes, my big little man." Why did Sammy feel the need to be so grown-up? Gabriella looked at him, really looked at him for the first time in a while and was surprised at what she saw. He was very serious to be so young. Where had all the little boy in him gone? She knew she was failing him, had been ever since Nicolas died, but she couldn't find the strength to make things right. Her insides had dried up, and what strength she may have had at one time was gone. *My God*, she thought. *How can I be so caught up in my own pain that I can't give Sammy what he needs? And what must Sammy think of me?*

She got up and cleared the table, and in a burst of optimism, told herself it wasn't too late to become the kind of mom Sammy needed. But after she stacked the dishes in the sink, she leaned against it and the reality of her world crashed down on her once again. Would this hopelessness that sucked away all her energy ever relent? Would she ever feel normal again? Wake up anticipating the day rather than dreading it?

"Mom?" Sammy's voice startled her as he brought his glass to the sink. "Can I help?"

"No, you run along."

He saw her wet eyes and wanted to say something, but instead turned and pretended not to notice. Her unhappiness was the reason he had to disobey her. If God could make his dad happy when he was so sick, maybe He could do the same thing for his mom. "Okay," he said. He didn't want to leave her, but he needed to be a man and make everything okay again. "I'll see you later," he said on his way out the door.

Sammy ran down the dirt path and ended up in the grove. He didn't stop until he came to his favorite tree. Sliding down the familiar trunk, he pulled out the handbill and read again that the revival was to take place on Sunday. It was only two days away. He pulled a pencil stub out of his pocket and began to list all the things he needed to do and pack for his mission. The revival was in Principios, a small town about ten miles down the coastline. Since he couldn't take the risk of anyone finding out about his disobedience, he'd have to walk, which meant he needed to leave pretty early Sunday morning. He might be able to find someone to give him a ride home after the revival.

"Hola, Samuèl. How are you?"

Sammy jerked his head up and then relaxed when he saw Raul walking toward him. He shoved the handbill and pencil into his pocket. "Hola señor. I'm good. And you?"

Raul didn't speak perfect English, but he liked to practice when speaking to Sammy. "I am still here," he said shrugging.

Sammy smiled, hopped up and followed Raul to his favorite resting spot—the end of an old wooden trailer that hadn't been used in years.

"I see you have the church paper. You will go, yes?"

Sammy sadly shook his head. "No, sir. My mom said no."

"Hmm," Raul muttered, shaking his head. "Why does your mother dislike God so much?"

Sammy shrugged. "I guess it's because she thinks it's His fault my dad died."

"Ah, yes."

"Is it?"

"Is what?"

"Is it God's fault my dad died?"

Raul took his time answering the question. Finally he said, "I think you need to talk to Padre Salinas from the church in the village."

"You think he'd know?"

Raul nodded. "Yes, I think he will."

Sammy wasn't so sure. He'd snuck down to the Colonia church a few times before and peered into the window while Padre Salinas preached. He was really old—older than even Raul and it looked to Sammy as if he'd had a difficult time staying awake while he spoke to the congregation. "I don't know."

"You want I should take you?"

Sammy was surprised at the hint of urgency in Raul's voice. He looked at him closely and couldn't help but notice the yellowed teeth that made Raul's smile so unique.

"I'm not sure," Sammy said. "Maybe later."

Raul shrugged it off, making Sammy think he'd imagined the urgency. "Bueno."

He felt bad for not taking Raul up on his offer, but he had a feeling about the revival. Sammy hoped he would find out what his dad had tried to tell him about before he died. He pushed his hand down into his pocket, touched the handbill and felt his stomach stir with the anticipation of something good on the horizon.

Later that night as Sammy laid in bed going over all the things he planned to pack for his trip, he heard a sharp "whack" on his window pane. He jumped up and without having to wonder where the noise had come from, yanked open the window and whispered. "Juan Jose! I'm here!"

"Vámanos!"

"Wait for me!" Sammy whispered. "I'll be out in a minute." Juan Jose, Sammy's best friend in the world, was always getting him into trouble. Juan Jose wasn't a bad kid, he was just a boy with an irrepressible curiosity and a penchant for always being in the wrong place at the wrong time. His mom had a habit of grounding him whenever he got into trouble, which was most of the time. This explained the late hour visit. Juan Jose had to sneak out of the house after his mom went to sleep if the two friends wanted to spend any time together.

Sammy lowered himself out of the window, and his feet thudded safely to the ground. When he and his mom first arrived in Rendiciòn, Sammy had learned Spanish quickly because of Juan Jose. His friend didn't understand one word of English, and Sammy, fresh from the U.S., hadn't known any Spanish. But the boys were the same age and instantly become best friends anyway. So Sammy devoured the language so he could communicate with him. Besides, he had to learn quickly because Juan Jose was the fastest talker he'd ever met.

Another reason they bonded together so tightly was because each of them had lost their dad at an early age. Sammy's died of cancer, and Juan Jose's left for the U.S. so he could try and earn more money to better support him and his mom. But after he left, they never heard from him again. The boys spent hours talking about what might have happened to him, and came to the conclusion that he would never have left on his own. Someone or something had to be preventing him from coming home, they decided, so the boys made plans to find him. They filled notebooks with detailed strategies outlining how they would rescue him once they found him.

But some kids from the village ruthlessly teased Juan Jose, telling him his father had deserted him and his mom. He refused to listen to them because his dad, just like Sammy's, was his hero.

"What's up?" Sammy asked as he landed in the dirt.

"Tango noticias de Maria" (I have news about Maria)

That instantly put Sammy on alert. Maria was the love of his life, and she was the girl he believed he was destined to marry. He'd known it the moment he first saw her six months ago when he spotted her at the market as she helped her father sell produce. She'd been bold, looking him right in the eye as she told him the price he offered for the bundle of cilantro was ridiculous. Every time Sammy thought about the fire in her eyes, he felt a longing to do something—to walk a little taller, try a little harder, to be a little more grown-up than he really was.

"What did she say?"

"She said..." Juan Jose took a deep breath, knowing that prolonging the answer was pure torture for Sammy. "Are you sure you want to know?"

"Juan Jose!"

"Bueno. She said she would hold your hand on three conditions," he said, speaking in his trademark rapid fire speech.

"Yes... go on."

"One. No one can be there to see. Two. You are not allowed to tell anyone. Three. When she says stop, you must let go of her hand."

Sammy released the breath he'd been holding. He couldn't believe she finally said yes. He'd been negotiating this event for months, primarily through Juan Jose because Maria refused to speak directly to him about it.

It drove him crazy every time he saw her at school or at the market with her father. She always smiled sweetly and pretended they weren't sending messages about the most important event of their lives. And now it was here. And it was really going to happen.

Juan Jose slapped Sammy on the back as they'd watched the grown men do a thousand times at the Plaza. "She said to meet her Sunday at the cove. You know the one?"

Sammy nodded. "Yes, I know where it is. I can't believe she finally said yes. What do you think changed her mind?"

"I'm sure it was my persuasive powers with the women."

Sammy laughed, grateful to have a good friend like Juan Jose. "There's something else," he said lowering his voice. He opened his fist to reveal the now tattered handbill. "I'm going."

"Your mamá, she said yes?"

Sammy slowly shook his head.

Juan Jose's eyes widened. "You mean…"

"I'm going anyway. I have to."

His friend nodded solemnly. Juan Jose had been on the bus the day Sammy watched his mom stand so close to the edge of the cliff and saw how scared he'd been. They'd talked about it many times after that day, and Sammy told him he thought God might be the answer to his mom's unhappiness. And so Juan Jose understood the importance of Sammy going to the revival so he could learn about the God his father had spoken of. He supported his friend's decision. "How will you get there? Raul?"

"No, it's too risky. I'm afraid he'll say something to my mom, so I'll have to walk."

"All the way to Principios? It will take hours!" he said hastily.

"I know, but…" He shrugged. "But it's the only way."

Juan Jose nodded knowingly. "I want to go with you, but it's too far. I'm sure my mamá would notice my absence after so many hours."

He waved his hands in excitement. "Hey, maybe I should go anyway! She'll only ground me some more."

Sammy wished his friend could go with him because he would feel a lot braver if Juan Jose were on the trip. But if he did, he'd be grounded the entire summer and it would ruin all their fun. "No, you better not. Anyway, I promise to tell you everything I learn."

Juan Jose hesitated a moment, then shrugged. "Bueno." He reached for the flyer to read it one last time before heading home to sneak back into his house. "Oh no," he said, his eyes widening again.

"What is it?"

"The date, Samuèl. It's the same day Maria has agreed to hold your hand!"

Chapter 4

The next morning Gabriella sat outside, swaying in the peeling, waterlogged porch swing—the same one her mother sat in so many years ago. She took a sip of the warm tea she'd brewed earlier and tried to relax. The smell of ripening oranges hung heavily in the air. She thought it ironic that the sweet, fragrant scent constantly surrounded her, invaded her senses, while her life consisted of nothing but bitterness.

The memories wouldn't leave her be.

"Gabby!" She heard her mother call out to her as if it were yesterday. "Stay where I can see you!"

She remembered looking over her shoulder at her mother and feeling the satisfaction that comes from knowing you're loved and safe in the world. She had wanted to push those boundaries, to see how far she could step out of bounds before her mother would rein her back in. Of course, the security she felt stemmed from knowing her mother would never let her go too far, and that's what gave her the confidence to venture out in the first place.

On some level, Gabriella had realized this on that day as she ran up to the porch swing where her mother sat. She wrapped her arms around her neck. "Te amo, mamá."

"I love you too, Gabby," she'd told her, laughing her tinkling laugh.

Gabriella, in a moment of absolute seriousness had put her tiny hands on both sides of her mother's face and turned it toward her until they were looking right at each other. "I never want to be without you," she said in her most serious tone.

Her mother smiled easily and shook her head. "Gabby, I will always be your mother. Wild burros couldn't drag me away from you."

But something had. And for most of her life, Gabriella had been left to wonder why she and her father drove away in the night, never to return.

She sighed deeply, turning her thoughts toward Nicolas and then Sammy. She always considered herself lucky that her aunt immigrated to Texas because it's where she eventually met Nicolas. And when they fell in love and married, she felt as if she were being given a second chance at a family. She had allowed herself to believe this one wouldn't disappear. And for a while, it looked as if her luck had turned, that she could finally relax and stop worrying that the people she loved would disappear from her life. But the relief hadn't lasted. While it was true that Nicolas hadn't disappeared into the night like her parents, he had left all the same.

God, or fate, or whatever it was that controlled things in this world had reached down from the heavens and snatched him away. She felt the disgust gnawing in the pit of her stomach. Again. And now Sammy was showing an interest in knowing this God and she didn't intend to allow it to go too far. There was just too much uncertainty, too many ways to get hurt. For instance, she reasoned with herself, if there were truly a God, the kind Nicolas spoke of, He must be a cruel one, and she wanted nothing to do with Him. She wouldn't allow her son to get sucked into the fairy tale either. He'd already been through enough.

Gabriella saw a swirl of dust in the distance which meant Mona, Raul's wife, would drive up at any moment. She put down her tea. It was time to get to work.

Mona pulled up in front of the house, throwing the dust up in a cloud. Gabriella watched as the door creaked open and Mona stepped out. Dressed in a plaid skirt and striped blouse—the dress of the old ones—she stood exactly 4 feet, 9 inches tall, although she told anyone who would listen she was 5 feet tall. Mona's face was broad, and she had a habit of scrunching up her features, which left the impression she was always contemplating something. Which she was. The thick black stockings she wore with everything bunched up and puffed out around her knees. She wore her husband's work boots. She was 71 years-old.

"Are you ready?" Mona asked in Spanish as she walked around to the trunk of her car and popped it open.

"As ready as I'll ever be," Gabriella said, walking down the steps to meet her. She looked into the jam-packed trunk, which contained an assortment of wood, tools and paint. A few days ago, Gabby and Mona had been drinking tea on the front porch when Mona made a comment about its condition. The salt water had all but eaten away the railing that bordered the wraparound porch, and she said it needed repair.

Gabriella agreed, but told her that until they harvested the grove, there wasn't any money to hire someone to fix it. When she and Sammy arrived three years ago, she had been speechless the first time she saw the house. Although she knew it hadn't been maintained since she left as a child, the condition of the house had shocked her because it was so different from the beautiful house she'd grown up in. She hadn't realized just how much money she'd have to put into it just to make it livable. Gabriella had invested much of her life insurance payout to get the house into shape, and had been living off of the rest since then. But most of the money was gone now, so she had to be frugal with what was left. She wished now she had redone the porch when she had the money.

She was thankful Raul had cared for the orange grove while she'd been gone. He told her he did it out of loyalty to her parents, but also because he loved the grove and didn't want to see it die. But he only kept it alive at a minimum, so when she came back they worked hard at fully restoring the trees health so they would once again produce the 300 oranges per tree she needed to make a living. This would be the first year the grove would produce an income large enough for her and Sammy to live on.

"You don't need to hire someone to fix the porch," Mona said. "We can do it ourselves."

"Us? But I wouldn't even know where to begin."

Mona waved her hand as if dismissing the thought. "Don't worry, I'll teach you."

And now here she was with a trunk load of unfamiliar looking things, and Gabby had absolutely no idea what to do with any of it. After they unloaded the supplies and put them on the porch, Mona handed Gabriella a paint scraper, took one for herself and they set their sights on neighboring poles on the far right side of the porch. After they'd worked in silence for a while, Mona spoke. "Gabriella?"

"Yes?"

"It's Raul. He asked if Samuèl will help him in the grove tomorrow. He's still not feeling well."

"Of course, he can. Sammy loves to work with Raul in the grove." She scrapped more paint and then stopped. "Raul's going to be all right, isn't he?"

Mona shrugged. "The doctor thinks it is his heart. But he doesn't know my Raul. His heart is strong. He just needs to rest some."

"Of course," agreed Gabriella.

Mona was right, she thought. Raul was strong, but he was also getting older and beginning to show his age. He'd always been a physical man, working with wood and then doing the hard labor the grove required. Now that his body was imposing new limitations on him, it must be for him. She wished she'd had the foresight to bring on another man to help him with the harvest this year.

They worked in the silence for a bit more, and then the memories got the best of her. "Mona?"

"Yes?"

"I... I don't know... I guess..."

"You want that we should take a break?"

"No, it's not that. It's just..." Gabby sighed, frustrated with herself. Why did she find it so difficult to talk about the things most important to her? Especially to Mona, who she considered to be her best friend.

She'd been pleasantly surprised when she returned to Rendiciòn to find that Raul and Mona were still around. Gabriella had quickly hired Raul to increase production in the grove to a level where it would support them, and he'd done an amazing job. She had vague memories of them from her childhood, and remembered they had not only worked for her parents, but were also their friends. And since she'd returned, she came to understand why.

The fact that Raul had made her parent's orange grove a labor of love for the past few decades had only deepened her affection for the couple. Over the past three years, she had grown close to them and considered them more than just employees—they were also her friends. In a way, Raul and Mona had become the family she'd always wanted.

But what she gleamed mostly from them were their stories—the pieces of her past she'd always longed to understand, but had no one to talk to about. She didn't know why she needed to hear the story again from Mona as if hearing it one more time could change things. But she always felt there was something she was missing, something she felt certain was there, in the telling, and it just hadn't yet come into focus. Still, she always held out hope that it would.

"You want I should tell you again?"

Gabby lowered her eyes and nodded.

Mona looked across the yard towards the grove and started speaking slowly. "Raul and I had been married for a few years when the woodworking shop he worked for went out of business. There weren't a lot of jobs here in Rendición, but we talked with a man at El Mercado who said the Juarez family, your parents, were hiring harvesters for a small orange grove. Now, Raul had no experience with oranges—he was a wood man—but you have to eat, no? So, he took the job. At first, the work was very difficult for him, but eventually Raul began to love the orange grove and developed a desire to learn as much about it as he could.

"Your parents were very kind to us and your father immediately took a liking to my Raul. He must have noticed Raul's interest in the work because he began to train him in the ways of the grove. By the end of two years, Raul had worked himself into the position of field boss, which was perfect timing because your mother became pregnant with you."

Mona stopped and looked closely at Gabriella. "You are okay?"

She nodded.

"Well, during this time I grew close to your mother. There were a lot of chores she couldn't do so we spent a lot of time together as she instructed me in how to do them. And your father? What a man for those times! He pampered her like a queen. He didn't want her to lift a finger the entire nine months. Anyway, as I said, I spent a lot of time with her, and I came to know her heart."

"And she was happy? About the pregnancy, I mean?"

"Oh, yes. She was so excited there were times she couldn't sit still for more than a minute. She planned every detail of your lives and spent many hours sewing clothes and blankets for you. When the time finally came, she was as big as a casa, and thrilled with the fact that she was about to have a child. I think she was a little afraid, too. She feared she wouldn't be a good enough mother, and then of course, the old women from the village had to tell her their own horror stories about the births of their children. Anyway, I tried to keep her away from them in the weeks before your birth."

Mona stopped for a minute and smiled as she remembered. "When the day came, she was so brave. Your mother began to get the pains early in the morning and I called Delores, the midwife. Now Delores was a very good midwife, but she could tell some horror stories about the birth like there's no mañana. So, after I called her, I watched out the window and when I saw her coming, I waited for her on the porch."

"You never told me this part of the story," Gabriella said. "Why did you wait for her? Were you worried about my mother?"

"Your mother? Oh no, she was doing fine, but I wanted to make sure I kept it that way. I didn't want Delores telling her any of the frightening stories right before the birth."

"So you waited to talk to her?"

"Talk to her? Delores? No, she was much too thick-headed for that. She's gone now, so you wouldn't know, but Delores never listened to anyone."

"So what did you do?"

"I threatened her."

"You what?"

"Yes. I realized the only way to protect your mother from the stress of those stories was to get through to Delores in the only way she would listen. Stress is bad for the babies, you know."

Gabby sat with her mouth open, shocked at what she'd heard. "But Mona… I guess I've never thought of you as a violent person."

"Me? Violent? Oh, no." She waved the thought away. "There were better ways to get through to Delores than with violence. You see, she had a horrible daughter who she wanted to find a husband for, and she finally found an older man who was willing to take her in. She had been trying to marry off the girl for years and was relieved she finally found someone who would put up with her. But I happened to know that every night the girl secretly met with Umberto, a fisherman's son who was pledged to someone else. If the truth came out, the older man wouldn't have married the girl and Delores would have been stuck with her forever."

"So you threatened to tell?"

"Yes. I warned her that if she told even one scary birth story, the entire town would hear about her daughter's indiscretion by sunset."

Gabby laughed. "Now that sounds like the Mona I know. What happened to the girl? Did she marry the older man?"

Mona nodded. "Yes, and then he took her to another village about four hours from here. Umberto never fully recovered."

"This isn't the same Umberto who works at the fish market, is it?" Mona nodded.

"Oh gosh," Gabriella said laughing. "I'll never be able to look at him the same."

"Well, your mother, she didn't hear one bad story on the day of your birth."

Gabriella looked wistfully at the grove, the smile still playing on her face. "How I long for those times. Crazy, fun days where family is all that matters. Days when the losses don't wear you down before you even have a chance to get out of bed."

"But things weren't always so perfect, even though we were all happy. This is also when a dark wind began to blow across our land."

Gabriella recognized the familiar sense of foreboding that always surfaced during this part of the story. She put down her paint scraper and listened intently.

"Rendición has always been a proud town," Mona continued.

"Proud of its hardworking people, its sense of family, and most of all, of its natural beauty. You can go for miles out to sea and still see the fish swimming near the bottom. As you've heard, many people believe our waters have healing powers because of its clarity. So when the owners of the oil tankers wanted to build a port in our village, many people were naturally against it because they thought the magic of the waters would be destroyed by the tankers. Your father was perhaps the most outspoken.

"At first, most people didn't want to get involved. I don't think they believed the tankers really wanted to dock in our small village. But when workers were brought in to begin constructing the docks, things changed very quickly.

"At first, the old men tried to sabotage the efforts by dumping the wood and tools into the sea at night. But the oil people would only bring in more. Some people called village meetings to discuss the problem, but the mayor continued to insist that progress was in everyone's best interest. We assumed he was only seeing the peso signs in front of his eyes.

"But then there was your father. He began to organize rallies and protests and more and more people joined the cause. Your mother supported him fully. In fact, there were plenty of times she stood next to him with you on her hip as he gave his rally speeches on an upturned crate.

"But don't think those days were only full of turmoil," she said. "Not at all. Your family was one of the happiest I knew, full of warmth, love and laughter. You were your father's little princess and your mothers best amiga. Oh, how the two of you could toil away the day in the garden, or spend all afternoon making an orange spice cake.

"But intertwined in those happy times were the threats and innuendoes that if your father didn't leave the tanker situation alone, it would get ugly."

"Do you think that's why they left? Did something happen to them out of their control?"

Mona shrugged. "All I know is this: they never would have left you willingly."

"But I saw them drive away," she said quietly.

"Ah, yes, Gabriella. This is the mystery, no?"

Just then, the front door swung open and Sammy walked out holding his backpack, which was stuffed full. "Uh… hi," he said, mid-step.

"Hello Samuèl. You are good?"

"Yes. And you?"

"Mona was telling me some stories," Gabby said. "Would you like to join us and help scrape the paint off these posts?"

"Uh… later, okay mom? I'm kind of doing something."

"Like what?"

"You know, stuff. But I'll see you later, okay?" And before she could answer, he disappeared back inside, slamming the door behind him.

"I don't like it," Mona said, "That boy—he is up to something."

"Oh, he's just being a kid," said Gabriella. "I'm sure he and Juan Jose are busy making plans for the summer."

Inside the house, Sammy closed the door and leaned against it. "That was too close," he whispered under his breath. His plan had been to get his bag outside and hidden underneath the porch, so that in the early morning hours when he planned to leave for Principios it would be one less thing he'd have to worry about.

He'd thought long and hard about what to do about the conflict between the revival and Maria and had finally come to the conclusion that if Maria were a reasonable girl—and he hoped she was because he planned to marry her one day—she would come to understand that sometimes there are things a man has to do. Be the man of the house. And this was one of those times.

Sammy had gone to Juan Jose's house earlier that day and asked him to give the message to Maria, along with a request for a new date. He tried to not think about her possible response. He had important things to do and he couldn't get distracted. Not even for Maria.

Earlier, he'd managed to sneak a box of crackers, a can of tuna and some jalapeno candy from the kitchen and it was neatly tucked away in his backpack. He didn't consider it stealing because it came from his own kitchen and he probably would have eaten it anyway. Especially the candy.

He also filled up two lidded glass jars with water from the sink and had even remembered to stuff toilet paper in the backpack just in case.

Finally, he placed a pen and a pad of paper in the bag because he'd promised Juan Jose he would tell him everything he heard. He wanted to write it down so he wouldn't forget it.

Now all he had to do was hide the backpack underneath the porch, decide which color Keds would be right for a revival—he had it narrowed down to red or orange—and figure out how to set the blasted alarm clock. He'd never done it before and couldn't find an instruction book anywhere. But he was no dummy, he'd figure it out.

Later that night, as Gabriella quietly opened Sammy's door to make sure he was sleeping soundly, she was surprised to find him sitting up by the window. "Sammy? Are you all right?"

She watched his shoulders shrug in the shadows of the room. "I guess so."

"Can't you sleep?" she asked as she padded across the room in her bare feet. She instinctively put her wrist to his forehead. "You don't have a fever. What is it?"

"Mom? Do you miss dad?"

Gabriella blew out her breath and sat down next to him on the window sill. "Sometimes I miss him so much I think my heart will break in two."

"Me, too. Mom?"

"Hmm?"

"Why did he have to die?"

She closed her eyes and steadied herself against the question she'd been dreading for a thousand years. "I don't know, Sammy. I wish I did."

"Do you think we'll ever get to see him again? Dad said if we found Jesus, we would go to Heaven, too. And then we could all be together. That's right, isn't it?"

Gabriella struggled within herself. She knew the answer she should give him, the one that would fill him with hope. If she were a different kind of mother, she would tell him that they would all be reunited one day in Heaven. But that would be a lie. One based on the imaginations of desperate men. On the other hand, it seemed just as cruel to tell him what she did believe. That his dad's life was over. That once a person died, there was a blank nothingness. But a small part of her wondered if someone as wonderful as Nicolas could simply cease to exist. If so, how could she ever explain this harsh truth to her son?

"Mom? Did you hear me?"

Gabriella looked at Sammy's soft features, which were just beginning to take on the defined characteristics of an older boy, and took the easy way out. "I don't know, Sammy. I wish I did."

An hour later, Gabriella stood on the edge of the cliff, shaking her fists violently at the sea. "Leave him alone," she shouted toward the sky. "You can't have him, too!"

Chapter 5

Sammy startled awake and looked at the clock. It was 3 a.m.—time to get moving. He'd been sleeping on and off for hours, afraid he'd miss his chance and not get to go to the revival. He toyed with the alarm clock the night before, but once he figured out how to make it work, he realized that it was loud enough to wake his mom, too. So he decided to stay up all night until it was time to leave, and except for a few short catnaps, he'd done it.

He rubbed his eyes, yawned and rolled out of bed. He quietly slipped into the clothes he'd laid out the night before and let himself out the window. Once he landed on the soft ground, he hesitated and again thought about whether he should leave his mom a note. He didn't want her to worry, but at the same time, if she knew where he was, she would probably come and get him and he would miss what the preacher said about God. After a few indecisive moments, he finally decided that he was doing the right thing because what he learned at the revival might make his mom happy again. So he gathered his backpack from underneath the porch and walked toward the road that would take him to Principios.

The darkness enveloped him, and for a moment he allowed himself to be overcome by fear. Sammy's mind went into overdrive as he remembered the stories he'd heard of the road between Rendiciòn and Principios. Juan Jose told him the road was filled with bandidos and wild dogs, and in a moment of panic, he realized that he hadn't brought anything with him to fight off a wild dog. He'd never done anything like this before. Was he making a mistake? If he were injured on the trip, it would give his mom something else to be sad about.

But then he looked up and saw the millions of stars in a protective canopy over his head and thought if he only had a ladder he might be able to touch them. He heard with crystal clarity the sound of the water racing recklessly toward the rocks and then crashing wildly into them. The night looked different away from the comfort of his house, and slowly the eerily crooked shadows of the trees, which had frightened him only moments before, transformed into peaceful and welcoming images. He stood up straighter and made up his mind to carry out his mission without fear.

When he reached the road, he saw Juan Jose running frantically toward him. "Samuèl, wait for me!" The sound of his friend's rapidly spoken Spanish shattered the silence so completely he was sure his mom could hear it a half mile away in her bed.

"Shh!" he whispered into the night. "What are you doing here?"

"I was afraid I missed you," Juan Jose said, bending over and holding on to his side. "I bring you news from Maria."

Sammy stopped, temporarily sidetracked from his mission. "Yes?"

"She said you broke her heart," he said, still trying to catch his breath. "And if you are truly a man, you will know what to do."

Sammy felt his heart flip flop in his chest. He thought of Maria and her dark eyes and the boldness that made him notice her in the first place. He didn't want to mess things up with her. But then the image of his mom standing on the cliff forced its way into his mind. And of the last time he had seen his father. So sick, but at peace because of this person named Jesus. And he knew. Even if it cost him his love, he had to do whatever he could to make his mom happy again. And that meant going to the revival. He just hoped Maria would eventually understand why he had to do it.

Sammy looked up at the endless sea of stars and realized the trip was about more than just his mom's happiness. He needed to hear this preacher, too. Someone made those stars, he thought, and he needed to find out who it was.

"What will you do?" Juan Jose asked, breathing a little easier now.

"You told her the part about me being a man and having to do something important?"

"Yes."

"And about me wanting to reschedule the date?"

Juan Jose nodded.

"And that I agree to all her conditions?"

"Yes, Samuèl. I told her everything."

"Then I don't understand. What does she want me to do?"

Juan Jose shrugged and kicked at the dirt. He picked up a rock and threw it at a darkened tree trunk. Barely missed. "Who can understand the mind of a woman?"

Sammy moaned inwardly and looked back toward his house. "Look, Juan Jose. Tell Maria I'm sorry I broke her heart and I really want to keep the date, but I can't cancel my plans for today. I am the man of my house and there are certain things I have to do. If she will just tell me how she wants me to make it up to her, I'll do it, okay?"

"Bueno. I'll take her the message."

"Thanks. I have to go."

"Don't forget," said Juan Jose. "You promised to tell me what you learn about God."

"I won't," said Sammy. "I packed some paper and a pen so I can write it all down." He started down the road. He was already tired, and he had a long way to walk.

Gabriella stirred from her sleep, something nagging at her subconscious. Was that a noise she heard? She listened groggily for a moment and decided it was nothing. She rolled over and went back to sleep. It was the weekend, and she planned to sleep in as late as she could.

Sometime later, Sammy felt something wet running down his back, so he stopped and sat on a big rock which was fine because he was tired and needed to take a break anyway. He looked at his watch, the one his dad left behind when he died, and was surprised to see he'd been walking for hours. Glancing toward the water, Sammy saw the daylight pushing itself up out of the sea and he was glad for the change. He'd had about all the darkness he could take.

He swung his backpack off his shoulder, brought it around and unzipped it. Everything was wet. The glass jars had leaked and were almost empty. Sammy thirstily drank down the remaining drops of water and tossed them aside. The paper he planned to use for Juan Jose's notes was soaked so he threw it out, too. The cracker box dripped with water, but luckily the crackers were in a plastic sleeve and had stayed dry. After tossing the box aside, he ripped open the plastic and shoved some crackers into his mouth. He hadn't planned on getting this hungry.

He tried to decide if he should eat the can of tuna or save it for later when he realized he'd forgotten to bring a can opener. Hungrily, he popped a jalapeno candy, which was only slightly soggy, into his mouth. He searched for a big rock, and when he found one he banged on the tuna fish can, trying to get it open. After ten minutes and not any closer to getting it open, he set it aside, frustrated. His stomach growled with hunger.

He felt heavy and weighed down and desperately wanted sleep. When he realized he was having trouble keeping his eyes open, he decided that if he could take a quick nap, he'd feel better and be able to pick up the pace on the rest of his journey. So, he took off his shirt, wrapped it around his dripping backpack and used it as a pillow. He was fast asleep within seconds.

Raul pulled up to the yellow house about 7a.m. He had decided today would be a good day to clear the paths between the trees to prepare for the harvest, and he hoped Samuèl was around to help. Before he reached the door, Gabriella stepped out with two cups of tea in her hand. "I saw the dust in the distance," she said. "Want to take a break before you get started?"

He smiled his yellow smile and accepted the tea gratefully. "Thank you."

After they sat down in the sea-sprayed chairs, Raul reached into his pocket and drew out an envelope. "Mona sent this for you."

Curious, Gabriella opened it and pulled out an old newspaper clipping. The photograph above the print was faded and barely discernable, but it looked like a shot of the sea with hundreds of black dots in it. There was also a large tanker off in the distance. She read the story quickly and then looked up in amazement. "I never knew about this."

Raul nodded. "I remember that day well. You want I should tell you about it?"

"Yes, please."

"Your father had been up and down the coastline photographing the damage the tankers had left behind in other villages. You see, our village was located at the halfway point of the trade routes and the tankers wanted to build a port and dock here. Some of the people saw this as a great opportunity to grow the village and become wealthy. But your father led a great amount of supporters and they put up quite a resistance, even though the opposition had more time and money to spend.

"But at the height of the disagreement, after the docks had been built, the tanker operators announced they would dock the following week. Your father's group was outraged because they weren't listening to them. They said they were going against the will of the majority of the people.

"So your father set up a watch system for the incoming tankers. Various people from the group were assigned to a specified lookout point at all times during the week, and when the tanker appeared, they were instructed to blow a horn. The sound of that horn set off a sequence of horns around the village and surrounding areas."

"Sounds pretty well organized."

"Organized yes, but also brave. Remember, these were mostly peasants and common laborers taking on the big oil companies."

"So what happened when the first tanker came?"

"It was early in the morning when the first horn sounded and soon you could hear horns blasting across the countryside. Hundreds of people streamed out of their houses, businesses, and wandered in from the country roads. They all gathered at the docks and at the command of your father, threw themselves into the sea. Some stayed near the docks, while others swam out farther, but every one of them played a part in blocking the tanker from docking."

"They won?"

"Yes. The tanker didn't dock that day, and every other time it tried to the horns would sound and people would come running to throw themselves into the tanker's path. It wasn't long before the oil companies built new docks at another village down the coastline."

"I bet some people were furious."

"Yes. People either loved or hated your father for it. There was no in-between."

Gabriella sat silent for a moment, considering the implications. Could this be reason enough for someone to have caused harm to her parents? She thought so, yes. Her heart swelled with pride for her father's plan—it was brilliant. And to think that his simple plan had brought big industry to its knees.

"I need to get to work," Raul said, interrupting her thoughts.

Gabriella's focus came back to the present. "Okay, but first, I wanted to ask—how are you feeling? Any better?"

Raul nodded. "Yes, I think I just needed a rest. I feel strong and ready to get back to work."

Gabriella smiled, relieved. "Good. I'll go get Sammy." She walked to the door and then turned and held up the clipping. "Thank Mona for this?"

Raul flashed his dingy smile and nodded.

Gabriella slipped inside. She hated to wake Sammy. He'd never slept this late, which meant he'd probably stayed up late into the night after their talk. But Raul needed help, and although he said he was feeling better, she wanted him to do as little as possible until the doctor cleared him completely. Anyway, she knew Sammy wouldn't mind. She quietly opened his door. Then, a minute later, she burst through the front porch door.

"Raul!" she cried. "It's Sammy! He's not in his bed!"

Chapter 6

When Sammy woke up from his nap he was hungry and frustrated because he was behind schedule. But at least he wasn't as sleepy anymore. He brushed off some ants from the remaining crackers and stuffed them and the jalapeno candy into his backpack. After he searched for and found the discarded glass jars, he was pleased to find a few remaining drops of water. He was so thirsty. Sammy put on his shirt, zipped his backpack and started walking down the road. He'd have to make double time to get to the revival before it ended.

Raul and Gabriella searched the property, they both agreed something was wrong. Sammy wouldn't just take off without telling her where he was going.

"I have an idea," Raul said. "Stay by the phone."

Raul intended to go to the one person who knew Samuél better than any person on earth. He slid behind the wheel of his battered truck and took off in haste down the road.

Gabriella went to Sammy's room for the hundredth time since Raul left. She was frantic with worry. Where could he be? She should have stayed with him last night and talked to him about the things keeping him awake. But instead, she'd retreated from his hurt, leaving him to deal with things on his own. *What kind of mother am I?*

She entered his room, sat on his bed and looked around. His things lie scattered around his room in the manner of a boy who has much more important things on his mind than orderliness. His baseball mitt and ball were casually tossed into the corner, and she was startled to see Nicolas' alongside Sammy's. She hadn't realized he'd kept it. Drawings of the rescue plans he and Juan Jose dreamed they would put into action once they found Juan Jose's father covered his desk, and his rock collection lay forlornly on his shelf. Where was he?

Gabriella rose and began to pace. She felt a longing, an urge to call out to someone, but who? She knew Raul would do whatever necessary to bring Sammy home, so what was this prompting she felt? Who did she know who could help?

Sammy heard the shouts and the gunning of the loud engine before he saw the truck. He pulled the backpack up higher on his shoulders and began to walk a little faster. He'd listened to stories about bandidos along this lonely stretch of road, but had always chalked them up to Juan Jose's vivid imagination. Now he wasn't so sure.

The roar of the engine grew louder, and it sounded like it was just around the bend. To be safe, Sammy ducked behind one of the many patches of underbrush that lined the road. The truck rounded the corner.

Sammy jumped as the rowdy young men in the jacked up red truck hollered and threw a beer bottle out the window as they went racing by. It skidded and then shattered, leaving glittering pieces of glass fanned out across the road.

Once the truck was out of sight, Sammy emerged. The men had scared him, and for the first time since starting out, he considered retreating back to the safety of his house. But then he thought about the promise he'd made to his dad. *No, I have to keep going. I'll just have to be more careful.* He continued on his way, this time keeping to the edge of the road, just in case the truck made another appearance.

Raul pulled up in front of Juan Jose's house, and when he got out of the truck, the pungent smell of goat meat cooking over an open fire wafted around him. Juan Jose's father, Rodolfo, had left his family a few years ago, telling them he was going to the United States to work so he could send them enough money to makes things easier for them, but he hadn't been heard from since. Despite the talk in the village, Raul knew the man and he didn't believe he would desert his family. Rodolfo was an honorable man, and he had spoken to Raul many times about his plans to make a better life for his wife and child. Since his disappearance, Juan Jose's mamá, Rosa, had experienced declining health. Some people attributed it to heartbreak while others felt her increased responsibilities were taking their toll. It was common knowledge in the village that Rosa's own father had left her and her mother in the same way, so most of the villagers were of the heartbreak opinion.

But either way, Rodolfo's absence affected her ability to raise Juan Jose in the best manner. Raul, along with some of the other old-timers from the village, lent her a helping hand when they could, but it was never truly enough.

Raul made his way up the porch steps and knocked on the door. When Rosa opened it, Raul was startled by her appearance. She looked like a woman in desperate need of a break. He silently scolded himself for not helping out more and promised himself he'd do more in the future.

But first, he had to find Samuél.

"Buenos dias, Rosa."

She smiled and pushed pack her limp hair. "Good morning, Raul," she said in Spanish. "Please come inside for some coffee."

He shook his head. "Gracias, but there's no time this morning. I'm looking for Juan Jose."

She eyed him carefully. "What has my son done, now?"

"Juan Jose hasn't done anything wrong. I'm hoping he can tell me where to find Samuél."

"Bueno." She turned her head toward the inside of the house and yelled. "Juan Jose! Come quickly!"

Moments later, a scruffy faced Juan Jose appeared at the door. "Raul! Did you come to help repair the chicken coop?"

"No, not today. I'm looking for Samuél. He's not at home, and his mother is worried. Have you seen him?"

Juan Jose looked at Rosa sheepishly, then back at Raul. "No, señor. I'm grounded, you see, so I've had no opportunity to see him."

"Ah, yes, I'd forgotten about that." He turned toward Rosa. "While I'm here, would you mind if Juan Jose showed me what's wrong with the coop? That way I'll know what to bring for the repairs."

As Raul and Juan Jose walked toward the coop, Raul put his arm around the boy's shoulders. "Samuél's mother is very worried. It's not like him to take off like this without telling her where he's going."

"No, señor."

"Are you sure you don't know where he is?"

Juan Jose thought it would be pointless to pretend he hadn't seen Samuél because Raul knew he snuck out of the house all the time to see his best friend. But he couldn't betray his confidence, either. The revival meant everything to him. But Raul had always been good to him and his mother, and he didn't want to lie to him. Frustrated, Juan Jose blurted out, "Please don't make me tell Samuél's secret. He'll never forgive me!"

Relieved, Raul bent down so they were face to face. "I know you want to do the right thing, but Samuél could be in danger. His mother is sick with worry."

Juan Jose looked at the ground, thought for a moment, and then looked up quickly, relief written all over his face. "I won't tell. But you can ask me questions and it would be wrong of me to answer them with lies."

Gabriella decided to bake orange glazed cinnamon rolls for Sammy's return and now found herself up to her elbows in flour and bread dough. She'd been trying to get out her frustration by pounding on the dough but it wasn't working. The nagging feeling that there was someone who could help wouldn't let up, which frustrated her all the more.

She put the dough in a large bowl and covered it with a dish towel to give it time to rise. Next, she went to the pantry to get the powdered sugar and orange oil for the glaze. When she opened the cabinet door, she heard something flutter on the back shelf and jumped. "Oh no," she muttered. "Not another mouse."

She dragged a chair to the cabinet so she could get a closer look and peered into the dark cabinet. *My gosh*, she thought. *I haven't seen this in years.* She moved aside various spices and cooking utensils and hesitantly pulled out what she'd found.

Nicolas's Bible.

She let out her breath, stepped down from the chair, and sat down. She eyed the Bible suspiciously and looked toward the ceiling. "You're trying to trick me, aren't you? Fine. If you're so all-knowing, tell me where my son is."

She closed her eyes, threw open the Bible and pointed. Then she cautiously opened her eyes and read right where her finger lie.

"'They took him and explained to him the way of God more accurately.'"

"Humph. Of course you don't know." She slammed the Bible shut and threw it aside. "Don't be an idiot," she scolded herself as she pulled down the powdered sugar. She glanced at the phone. Where was Raul?

Raul turned the ignition key and pointed his truck toward the road. It hadn't taken too many questions to figure out Samuél had gone to the revival against his mother's wishes. He was mad at himself for not figuring it out sooner. After all, Sammy had been reading the flyer in the grove only yesterday. Raul was both pleased and worried. Pleased that the boy taken an interest in the things of God—he'd felt a curiosity about it himself lately. But the isolated stretch of road leading to Principios was a dangerous one. Full of bandidos and wild dogs. Not a place for a sheltered young boy to be alone. Raul pushed down on the gas pedal and willed the truck to go faster.

Sammy heard two things at once: the roar of the menacing truck and a sweet music that sounded like it was coming from a loud speaker. The revival! He ducked behind some brush, but not before the truck came to a squealing halt.

"Gringo!" A drunken man called. "We can see you!"

Sammy, his heart thumping wildly in his ears, tore off down an overgrown dirt path that ran parallel to the road. He heard the truck doors slam and the men laughing and calling out to him. He ran with all his might. Before long, he had to drop his backpack because it was slowing him down by thumping so hard against his back. He stopped for a moment, bent over and tried to catch his breath. They were still back there. He could hear their ragged breathing as they tore through the brush. "God," he whispered, "if you're really up there, please don't let them catch me."

He saw a blur of black, one of the men's T-shirts, coming directly at him. There was no way he could outrun all of them, so he quickly ducked under a thick patch of brush and crawled as far as he could into the briars. The thorns ripped and tore at his clothes and skin, and Sammy hoped his blue T-shirt wouldn't give him away. When he reached what he thought was the center of the thicket, he curled himself up into a tight ball and waited.

Chapter 7

An hour later, bleeding, hungry, thirsty and exhausted, Sammy finally stood outside of a large white canvas tent. The men had looked for him for what seemed like hours, but the alcohol coursing through their veins eventually got the best of them. And in the end, they gave up the hunt.

But now Sammy had a problem. In his panic, he'd lost control of his bladder, and a large, wet stain had spread across the front of his pants. There was no way he could go inside that tent.

Furious with himself and too ashamed for anyone to see him, he sulked around the side of the tent where he could still clearly hear the voice of the preacher.

"Are you looking for something, but aren't sure what it is?" the preacher boomed. "Do you constantly try to fill that longing with people or things, but they never quite seem to satisfy you?"

Sammy sank to the ground and leaned up against the tent. It was hard and taunt against his back.

"Are you aware that when you were created, God left a large hole in the center of your heart that only He can fill? But some people try their entire lives to fill it with relationships or work or shopping or food or alcohol. But it never quite works, does it? You're always left wanting for more."

Sammy listened intently. Is this what his dad had come to know? Had he filled up the hole in his heart? Is that why his mom always seemed to be so unsatisfied? Like something wasn't quite right? He placed his hand over his own heart. Does this explain the mysterious longing he'd felt for as long as he could remember?

"I'm telling you, you can fill this hole today. But first, there's something you should know."

Sammy sat up straighter, forgetting about his hunger and thirst and the dirt caked to the front of his wet pants.

"If you make Jesus Christ the Lord of your life, He'll absolutely wreck it!"

Sammy heard the audience gasp.

"Don't think the Creator of Heaven and earth is some feeble God who will allow you to invite Him halfway into your life. Don't think you can call yourself a follower of Christ and not follow Him. Christ isn't for the fainthearted, and He's not for those of you who want say a little prayer and then go on with your lives as if nothing has changed. He is the Lion of Judah, The Lord of Lords, and the King of Kings! And I'm telling you He will turn your life upside down! He's the great I AM!"

Sammy heard the rustle of people inside and then saw a few of them walking down the path that led away from the tent.

"Now before any of you begin to think He's asking too much of you, let me tell you why He has the right to do so."

Sammy was excited about what he was hearing, but also terrified. He wanted to know what it would be like if the longing in his heart was filled, but he didn't understand what the preacher meant when he said Jesus would wreck his life. Is that why his dad died after he'd found Jesus? Would he die, too? His stomach growled, and he licked his lips to get rid of the awful dryness in his mouth. But he put his uncomfortableness out of his mind and instead listened to what the man inside the tent had to say.

Raul finally reached Principios and followed the noises to the revival tent. Hundreds of people gathered inside the tent and he wondered how he would ever find Samuél. Hesitantly, he walked in and took in the scene before him. A long wooden stage that looked like it had been hastily constructed sat at the back of the tent. On it was a lumbering man who looked vaguely familiar to Raul. He looked to be in his sixties, and stray strands of his salt and pepper hair whipped to and fro as he moved heavily back and forth across the stage. He wore dark brown trousers and a green long-sleeve shirt held up by tan suspenders. Even as the man moved back and forth across the makeshift stage with his voice booming over the loud speaker, he had a calm about him. Like the eye of the storm. The gray, opaque stillness before the crack of thunder.

A few hundred people sat in mismatched chairs, and more stood in the rear of the tent. They appeared to be listening intently. Their rapt attention was on the stout speaker on stage.

"Jesus Christ has the right to every area of your life because he died an excruciating death for you."

Raul moved along the back wall, keeping an eye out for Samuél while listening to the preacher.

"The God of this universe willingly came down to this planet as an infant with the intention of sacrificing Himself so He could one day be in a relationship with you and me."

Raul slid his eyes toward the preacher. *Did I hear him right?*

"You see, God didn't create the world like it is today with all the sickness, violence, dying and meaningless. No, He created a perfect world, but Adam and Eve, the first people to populate the earth, sinned against Him by wanting to be equal to Him rather than serving Him as their God. When they did that, a great separation occurred between mankind and our Creator. Now humans seemed to be all right with that separation. They went their own way and did whatever seemed right in their own eyes."

Raul watched a couple get up from their seats and walk out, shaking their heads in disgust. Was Samuèl here somewhere?

"But were they really all right?" the preacher asked the audience. "They murdered as a way to get what they wanted. People built idols to bow down to so they could act pious while asking for what they wanted, all the while truly serving no one but themselves. They became sexually promiscuous in search of a love they could only find in their Savior.

Friends, people have been trying to fill that hole in their hearts since the great separation, but no one's ever been able to do it with anything other than God.

"You see, God doesn't want us to go through life looking for something we can never find. He didn't create us to live apart from Him."

Raul slid down the wall until he was sitting on his haunches. He was no longer scanning the crowd for Samuél, but had become mesmerized by the man's words.

"But the only way to end the separation was with the ultimate sacrifice. God allowed Himself to be killed—hung on a cross like a common criminal—because the longing in His heart was so deep for you and for me, and it was the only way for reconciliation. Listen to what I'm saying, friends," the man said in a softer voice. "God died a cruel and unthinkable death because He—the one who can create whatever and whoever He wants with one breath—misses us. Wants to be in relationship with us. Does it sound like He's earned the right to be called the Lord of your life?"

Raul looked around the tent and saw that some people in the audience were crying, while others sat with their arms crossed, looking bored.

"You might ask why it had to be this way, why Jesus had to die," said the preacher. "Understand please that the God of the universe is holy. It is impossible for Him to be in relationship with sin. But the Bible says we've all fallen short of the glory of God. Every one of us, no matter how many times you've sat in a church pew, or how many good deeds you've done, are still a sinner in the eyes of God.

"You see, because of what Adam and Eve did in that garden, humans are born with a sinful nature." The man looked out into the crowd. "What? You don't believe it? How many of you had to teach your young children to lie or sneak candy when they thought you weren't looking? Sin is a part of the human condition, and God simply can't be in its presence.

"But cheer up! Jesus said that He is the Way, the Truth and the Life, and no man gets to the Father, who is in Heaven, except through Him. Praise be! He's made a way!"

Sammy roughly wiped away the tears, unaware of anything around him. It wasn't fair that God had to die just because people messed up so badly. He thought about all the things he'd done wrong in his life, like being here in defiance of his mom, and he cried even harder. In that moment, Sammy was sure his dad had made the right decision, even if God took him to Heaven because of it. He thought it was only fair. He knew he wanted this Jesus to fill the hole in his heart, even if it meant dying like his dad. If it were possible to love someone you'd never even met, Sammy had just fallen hopelessly in love.

"But the good news doesn't end there," the preacher said. "You see, Jesus is God, and not even the sins of the whole world were enough to keep Him down. The third day after He died on that cross and was given up for dead, he startled the world by getting up and walking out of the tomb. That's right, he just walked out."

The preacher peered out into the crowd. "What? It's too unbelievable? Your faith can't stretch that far? Ha!" He paced back and forth across the stage. "Is death too hard for the Creator of Life? If you believe He gives life, why wouldn't you believe He can take it away at will? No, the difficult thing, the unfathomable idea is that His motivation for this entire scenario was love. Love for you and love for me.

"Now, if your heart tells you that you're ready to ask God for forgiveness of your sins and repent—that means turning away from them—and you want to accept His offer of eternal life with Him in Heaven, I want you to come down here and we'll tell Him together."

Raul was halfway down the aisle before he even he knew what he was doing. Why hadn't anyone ever told him this before? He thought of the few times he'd gone to church back in Rendiciòn and wondered why Padre Salinas hadn't spoken of it. He glanced around, hoping to get a glimpse of Samuél. Had he heard the message, too?

Sammy sat debating. He wanted more than anything to be with God, but he thought about the promise he'd made to his dad. That he would take his mother with him to Heaven. Maybe he would have more time than his dad did before he died. That way he would have the chance to explain things to her. And Juan Jose. And Raul and Mona.

"Before we pray, I want to wait one more minute. I feel like there's someone here who wants to come, but isn't here yet."

Sammy scrambled to his feet and ran around the tent toward the entrance. "I'm coming Jesus," he mumbled as he ran. "Please let me tell my mom and friends about you before you take me to Heaven."

When Sammy entered the tent, he saw that half the chairs were empty and a big group of people were crying and kneeling by the stage. He started toward it. As he walked, tears streaming down his face, he locked eyes with the preacher.

"Yes son, come down here. Jesus has special plans for you. I can sense it."

Sammy looked around and then he realized the man on stage was talking to him. When he looked back toward the preacher, the man had closed his eyes and lifted his hands toward the ceiling. It didn't matter. All Sammy wanted was Jesus.

He stopped at the rear of the crowd and knelt down on his knees. He braced himself. These might be his last few breaths on this earth.

"Let's pray," said the preacher.

Sammy repeated every word and meant it with everything in his heart. The tears kept coming and slowly, he felt the hole in his heart begin to fill up. He stopped listening to the preacher, stopped repeating his words, and instead, told Jesus everything in his heart. The tent and all the people in it faded to the back of his consciousness, and at that moment, Jesus was the only one who mattered.

And then he felt it. Loved beyond measure. Forgiven. Complete.

"I'm coming, Jesus" he whispered. He squeezed his eyes shut and waited to die.

Mona pulled up to the yellow house and slammed on her brakes, sending the dust flying. A moment later, she stepped out of the car with her brightly colored floral shirt and brown pinstriped skirt. Black leggings with the poufy knees.

"Oh Mona," Gabriella cried, racing down the steps to embrace her. "Where could they be? Now they've both disappeared."

Mona shook her head and set her jaw stubbornly. "My Raul is a smart man. He will find Samuél."

After a few minutes, Sammy heard noises and cautiously opened his eyes. Was it possible he was still alive? He reached down and pinched his leg and when it smarted, he knew it was true. Slowly, he scanned the room, and realized that everyone else who prayed to Jesus was still alive, too. Maybe it wasn't instantaneous after all.

"Samuél!"

"Raul!" Sammy jumped up and ran toward him. "Raul, you're here! I'm so glad you came!"

Raul watched as Sammy ran toward him. He was sure he'd heard the message too because he could see it in his eyes. They would have much to talk about on the way home. But Samuél looked a mess. Tears streamed down his dirty face, and his pants were caked with wet, sticky dirt. His blond curls were wild, sticking out in all directions, and there were scratches and dried blood along his arms and face. He limped a little, and Raul imagined it was from walking such a long distance. As he got closer, he saw that Sammy's lips were parched and shriveled.

"Raul, did you hear?"

He nodded, wanting to rejoice with the boy, but his mind was heavy with the fact that his disobedience had caused Gabriella so much pain and worry.

Sammy looked down. "You're mad at me, aren't you?"

Raul let out a long breath. "Samuél, your disobedience has given us much to be happy about." He looked toward the stage, empty now, but for a few men breaking it down. "But your mother? She is very worried. She will be angry when you get home."

"I know. But Raul, I had to know."

He closed his eyes and nodded.

Sammy reached up and touched Raul's heart, and then he looked at him questioningly.

He smiled. "Yes, Samuél. My heart was also filled."

It was dark now, and in an effort to calm Gabriella's fears, Mona pulled out the tools she'd brought the day before, and insisted they take out their frustrations on the rotting wood of the porch poles. The sound of scraping against the quiet of the night was grating on both of their nerves. The mosquitoes were out and every few minutes, Gabriella or Mona would slap at one, which was the only interruption in the monotony of the work. Both women were quiet, each afraid to voice the fears that were running rampant in their minds.

The shrill ring of the phone cut sharply into the night.

Gabriella threw down her scraper and ran into the house. "Hello!" she yelled into the phone, out of breath from racing to answer it. "Raul? Is that you?"

"Yes," he said. "And I have Samuél with me."

She sagged into the chair, relief washing over her like a summer rain after a long, hot drought. "Is he okay? And you?"

"Yes. He needs to eat and drink. And then we will drive home."

She nodded, giving Mona the thumbs up to let her know they were both all right. "Where did you find him? Where was he?" She heard a deep sigh on the other end of the phone.

"Maybe it would be better if he tells you when we get there."

"No, Raul. I need to know now. I can't take any more stress tonight."

"Bueno." He hesitated. "I found Samuél at the revival in Principios."

Gabriella dropped the phone and ran out of the house, but not before picking up Nicolas' Bible and violently throwing it into the trash.

Chapter 8

Sammy shoved the fifth taco into his mouth and guzzled down his third glass of water. Finally, he came up for air. "Raul? Do you believe we'll have time to tell others about Jesus before we go to Heaven?"

"I guess so, yes. Why wouldn't we?"

"Well, my dad didn't have much time. I mean, does God take all of us to Heaven right after he fills our hearts, or just some of us?"

"You think we are going to die because we made Jesus our Lord?"

Sammy nodded. "Isn't that what the preacher said? That Jesus would wreck our lives? It happened to my dad."

"Yes, but I think your father found out about God before he died. He didn't die because God filled his heart."

"But the preacher said Jesus would take us to Heaven."

"Yes, Samuél, but that won't happen until you are an old man."

"Ohhhh."

"You mean to tell me you thought you would die when you made Jesus Christ the Lord of your life?" a booming voice asked.

Startled, Raul and Sammy turned to find the preacher from the revival standing behind them. "I'm sorry, I didn't mean to scare you, but I couldn't help overhearing your conversation." His brown eyes danced and finally lighted on Sammy. "Did I hear you correctly, son?"

Sammy looked down, embarrassed. "Uh… yes, sir."

"Mind if I have a seat?" he asked as he settled himself onto the stool next to Sammy. "So, you were willing to die for the Lord? Just like that?"

Sammy looked at the preacher and saw that his eyes had the same light his dad's had before he died. "What choice did I have, sir? I mean, after what He did for me?"

"Well, I'll be."

Mona caught up with Gabriella along the shoreline. She stood back and watched her shake her fists at the sea, then pick up whatever she could find and violently throw it towards the water. Mona was surprised someone so tiny could throw with such force. As she watched Gabriella exhaust herself and sink to her knees, Mona saw that her peasant skirt and loose blouse were soaked through with sweat. *I should have brought a blanket to cover her with.*

Mona started toward her to offer some comfort, and as she neared, she heard Gabriella angrily talking out loud. "Why won't you let us be? Haven't you taken enough?" She picked up some sand and weakly threw it toward the sea. "Just go away and leave us alone. We don't want you."

"Gabriella," Mona said, kneeling down and wrapping her arms around her. "Nobody is going to take Samuél from you. Raul found him safe and he is bringing him home now."

"From the revival," she muttered. "He went to find out about God." She spat out the last word.

"Yes. But he is just a boy. Soon he will forget this nonsense."

"You don't understand."

"Yes, Gabriella, I do. More than you know."

Gabriella stared at the dark churning water. "I hate Him, Mona. He's taken away everyone I've ever loved." She shook her head. "He can't have my Sammy, too. I won't allow it."

The preacher accepted the glass of water from the man behind the counter and held up four fingers when asked how many tacos he wanted. "I meant what I said in the tent, son. I sense that God has a special calling on your life." He leaned into the counter and peered around Sammy at Raul. "Is he your grandson?"

Raul shook his head. "It feels like he is, but no" he said, reaching past Sammy to shake the preacher's hand. "Have we met before?"

"They call me Preacher," the man said, roughly shaking Raul's hand. "You do seem familiar to me, but I can't quite place you."

He turned back toward Sammy. "How old are you, boy?"

"Ten." He held up his pointer finger. "Almost eleven."

"Almost eleven, huh?" He leaned back to get a closer look. "Where are your parents?"

"My dad… well, he died and went to Heaven. And my mom? I live with her in Rendición."

"I hope she's got a heart to understand what the Lord's going do with your life, son."

"No, sir."

"No?" He looked past Sammy at Raul.

"Samuél's mother doesn't like the things of God. In fact, she forbids them. He came here against her wishes."

"Well, I'll be," he said, sitting back and taking it in. "I'm afraid she may be in for a surprise."

"What do you mean?" Sammy asked.

"What I mean," said the preacher, leaning his barrel-like body in towards Sammy. "Is that when God puts a call on a man's life, there not much anyone can do about it. Not even a mama."

The next morning, Gabriella was up before the sun. She'd been awake most of the night thinking about how Sammy had gone to the revival without her permission, and after the restless night, she believed she knew what caused his uncharacteristic disobedience. "Sammy," she called. "Get up so you can have breakfast before Raul gets here."

"Okay, mom." Sammy lay still for a moment, preparing for the day. The night before when he and Raul had driven up to the house, his mom and Mona had been waiting for them. Mona immediately gave his mom a hug and then walked to her car, calling out to Raul that she'd see him at home.

His mom had stood on the porch waiting, hands on her hips. Sammy had looked to Raul for help, but he looked just as scared as he was. "Here goes," Sammy mumbled under his breath.

"Vaya con Dios," Raul whispered.

His mom waited until he reached the porch and then reached out to hug him firmly. "I was worried about you, Sammy."

He hugged her back tightly. "I'm really sorry Mom, but—"

"—We'll talk about it in the morning," she said as she pulled away. "Now, go get a shower and get in bed. You and Raul start in the grove early tomorrow morning."

"Yes, ma'am."

He turned to go inside, confused because his mom was acting so calm. He had expected her to scream at him, or at least be crying when he got home because he had scared her. But instead, she'd hugged him. On the way into the house he'd turned around to tell her he was sorry but saw that she'd gone to Raul's truck to talk to him. And now she was calling him for breakfast just like everything was fine. Was his punishment coming now?

He pushed out of bed and pulled on some clean clothes. He began straightening his room by putting away some clothes in the dresser and books on the shelf. Anything to delay what was coming.

"Sammy!" she called again from the kitchen. "Your cinnamon rolls are ready!"

Sammy dropped the book he'd been holding. *Cinnamon rolls? She fixed my favorite breakfast? What in the world is going on?*

Cautiously, he made his way toward the table. "They smell really good, mom."

"Thank you." She brought a steaming plate of doughy rolls to the table. "Let me get you some cold milk to go with these."

Sammy looked at her closely. Even though she was smiling and pretending everything was okay, he could see that it wasn't. Her face looked tight, like it did when she was mad, and the dark circles under her eyes looked like someone had colored black smudges on her face.

But what really stood out were her eyes. He peered into them, but no matter which angle he looked at them from, the light he'd seen in other people's eyes last night wasn't there.

"Sammy, why are you looking at me like that?"

He shrugged and took an enormous bite out of his roll. "Yummy. These are great, mom."

She settled in across from him and folded her hands on her lap.

Here it comes, he thought.

"Sammy, I want to apologize."

He dropped his roll and the sticky orange glaze glopped onto his forearm. He quickly picked up the roll and licked the glaze off his arm. "You what?"

She got up, ran a dishtowel under the warm water, and handed it to him. "I said I want to apologize."

"For what?"

"For not being the kind of mom I should be."

He was about to respond, but she held up her hand. "Hear me out, Sammy. At first, I was very angry about what you did yesterday, but then I thought about why you did it."

"Mom, I—"

"—Now, Sammy, you can have your turn when I'm finished speaking, okay?"

"Yes, ma'am."

"I realized that the only way you would do something so dishonest is if you were searching for something you felt was missing."

"Exactly!"

She nodded and smiled. "So that's why I want to apologize. Ever since your dad died, I've been so caught up in my own grief and confusion, and, well… I just haven't been a very good mother to you. But all that's going to change now, I promise. I'll go back to being my old self, and you can put aside this God thing."

"Put aside God?"

She nodded. "Really, Sammy. I know you were missing something in your life, but I'm telling you, I'm going to be a better mom. You'll, see. Everything will be okay again."

Sammy sat stunned for a moment. "Mom, you think I went to the revival to learn about God because you've been sad about dad?" His face twisted in confusion.

"That's right." She got up and carried his now empty plate to the counter.

"But mom, there's something you don't understand."

"Oh good, here's Raul now," she said, looking out the window. "Take out the trash on your way out, okay?"

"Mom?"

"Yes?" she asked as she washed the breakfast dishes.

"Only God can fill up the hole in a person's heart. And mine got filled last night."

Sammy took out the trash like his mom asked him to. It was pretty obvious his last remark had shaken her up, and she wanted to be alone with Raul. He was sure they were talking about him.

As he lifted the bag to put it in the outside garbage can, he spotted a big brown book in the bottom of it. *What's this?* He punched a hole in the bag near the book and pulled it out. A Bible? He opened the front cover and gasped at what he saw. His dad's name. On a Bible. His dad's Bible. He found his dad's Bible! He scraped away the clinging trash and hugged it close to his chest, feeling like he'd found the best treasure in the world. But wait... why was it in the trash?

He looked back toward the house and the only person who could have thrown it away, and very slowly, a terrifying question crept into his mind. What happens to people who die without asking Jesus to fill the hole in their heart?

Sammy joined Raul and his mom in the grove as soon as he'd hidden the Bible underneath the front porch. He had vague memories of his dad reading it after he got sick. He used to call it "The Word of God." Sammy wondered if it held the answers to his many questions.

"We're over here, Samuél!"

He made his way toward the first row in the grove where Raul and his mom were busy clearing rocks and limbs from the path. After picking up some of the debris, Sammy added it to the growing pile. He tried to catch Raul's attention, and after a few tries, the man looked his way. Sammy pointed to his mom, who was carrying a load of limbs to the pile, and whispered, "She doesn't understand! She thinks it's her fault I went to the revival!"

"Yes," Raul whispered. "We must pray."

Pray? Sammy thought. *About that? Would God really be interested in a prayer about a misunderstanding between me and my mom?* He thought back to when he'd emptied out his heart to God in prayer and how good it had made him feel. He wasn't sure if it was the proper way to pray, but he decided to give it a try and carried on a conversation with God while he worked.

After a few hours, Gabriella declared it was time for a break and they each plucked an orange and sat down on the old wooden trailer.

"There is nothing in the world like the smell of a sweet orange," said Raul. "It's one of the reasons I refused to let this grove die after you left."

Gabriella nodded, enjoying her own cool, fragrant orange. "I can't imagine how much harder it was to maintain when the grove was twice this size."

"The orange grove used to be bigger?" asked Sammy.

"Yes, it did. But a fire broke out and destroyed half of it when I still lived here as a child."

"What started the fire?"

Gabriella shrugged. "I don't think anyone ever knew. It was an accident of some sort."

Raul raised his eyebrows. "Is that what you think?"

"You don't?"

He sighed deeply, and then slowly shook his head. "I don't really have the answer, but there was a lot of talk after the fire. Some people believe Hector Mendez is the person who burned down the grove."

Gabriella sat up straighter. "Hector Mendez? The man who owns the bank in town?"

"Yes."

"But why would he burn down the grove?"

"People said he did it because of the tankers."

"The tankers? I don't understand."

Raul ate the last segment of his orange, then leaned back on his hands. "You understand that this was just the talk in the village? I don't know what really happened."

She nodded, urging him on.

"Many people were angry about the support your father rallied against the tankers. The people who wanted the tankers to dock here were excited because if Rendición became a port city, it would grow and that meant more jobs and more opportunities for business. It meant building new houses, opening more shops, and the people who lived here would sell more of their produce and products."

"And as a banker, I guess Hector Mendez stood to gain financially more than anyone else."

"Yes."

"But that's one thing I don't understand, Raul. Why was my father so opposed to the growth? Surely he was concerned about more than how the docks would affect the look of the coastline."

Raul nodded. "Yes, there was more to it than that. He talked about two reasons for opposing the tankers. The first was the issue of the environment. The oil tankers had a history of polluting the areas where they docked, and your father didn't like the idea of that. But it wasn't only the natural pollution he feared."

"What else was he worried about?"

Raul looked at Sammy, then down at his shoes. "Your father said the pollution wouldn't just be limited to the environment." He looked at Gabriella. "Are you sure you want to know?"

She nodded.

Raul hesitantly continued. "As you can imagine, when the tankers docked in a port, they brought more with them than just pollution and potential oil spills. Many of the men on such ships led a certain lifestyle." He glanced in Sammy's direction and then put his hands over the boy's ears to keep him from hearing. "In the other port cities many bars, liquor stores and houses of prostitution popped up. And of course, that caused the crime to go up, too," he whispered.

"I'm almost eleven, you know." Sammy said indignantly. Raul took his hands off of his ears.

Gabriella patted Sammy's leg and then tossed aside her orange peel. "I guess I can understand my father's concerns. It just sounds awfully…"

"Christian?"

Gabriella's head snapped up. "What are you saying, Raul?"

"Gabriella," he said, his voice soft and careful. "There are many things you do not know."

"My parents were not Christians."

"Not at first, no."

She stubbornly shook her head, stood up and walked away. She hadn't gone far when she spun around, her petite body trembling with emotion. "I will not have you smear the memory of my parents. They were good, decent people, not fools who believed in fairy tales."

"Not fools, no," he said gently. "But people who had come to believe in God and His morals."

Gabriella stared at him, her dark eyes burning. "If that were true, I would have some memory of it."

He shrugged. "Of this I do not know. I'm only telling you what I saw and heard."

She stood there for a while until the anger passed, and then she cautiously took her place at the end of the trailer. "I'm sorry, Raul. I'm not upset with you, but you must be remembering wrong."

He smiled, his teeth dingy in the sun. "It's okay."

"Please, tell me more about Hector Mendez. Why do some people think he burned down our grove?"

Raul nodded, thankful she wasn't angry with him. "On the day the tankers were scheduled to dock here for the first time, Hector planned a grand welcoming party for the crew. He set up booths with food and drinks, and a large crowd of people who supported the tankers gathered for the celebration. It was supposed to be their victory party because they were sure they had won the fight."

"But my father and his supporters thwarted them by jumping into the sea so the tankers couldn't dock," she said.

"Yes. And that day Hector swore he would get revenge on your father. The grove was burned the next week."

Gabriella thought for a moment. "And how much longer after that did my parents disappear?"

"Exactly one month later."

Gabriella shook her head in disbelief and stood up. "Hector Mendez, huh? Has he been here ever since? He never left?"

"He's owned the bank the entire time. The only way he'll ever leave Rendición is through the death."

She nodded resolutely. "I'm going to make us some lunch. I'll ring the bell when it's ready."

Sammy waited until his mom was out of earshot, and then asked, "Did my grandparents really believe in God?"

"Yes."

"But how do you know? I mean, if my mom didn't, how do you?"

"Because Mona and I were working the night your parents had a visitor—a man who came to tell them about Jesus. They tried to tell me about it later, but at the time, I didn't want to hear it."

"But why?"

"Because I thought it was a trick."

"Why?"

"Because the man who came to talk to them about God was an acquaintance of Hector Mendez."

"But he was a man of God?"

"I do not know about then, but now he is—of this I am sure."

"How?"

"Because I met him again last night. He is the man called Preacher."

Chapter 9

Later that night, Sammy heard the familiar thunk on his windowpane. He threw off his covers, jumped out of bed and ran to the window. He'd been waiting for his friend for what seemed like hours. "I'm here, Juan Jose! Wait for me!"

Sammy lowered himself out of the window and jumped down to the dirt, where he found a subdued Juan Jose. "What's wrong?" he asked when he saw his downtrodden face.

"I'm sorry," Juan Jose said in his hastily spoken Spanish. "I didn't tell Raul where you were, but he guessed, and I couldn't lie to him. Can you ever forgive me?"

"It's okay, I'm not mad at you. And I'm really happy Raul showed up because the most amazing thing happened to us."

"You're not mad at me?"

"Of course not. I wouldn't have been able to lie to Raul either." He glanced nervously toward the house. "Let's go to the grove. I have so much to tell you!" They hurried away from the house so their voices wouldn't travel through the windows and into his mom's bedroom to wake her up. Sammy took him to his favorite orange tree. The wind played in the tree's branches, running through them like an excited child playing in a field full of tall grass.

"Sit here, I'll be right back." Sammy left his confused friend and ran to the porch where he'd hidden his dad's Bible. He crawled under the porch, retrieved the book and carried it reverently to his friend.

"Bueno," said Juan Jose when Sammy sat down. "Tell me everything."

And so he did. He told him about the mishaps along the way, the horrible hunger and thirst he'd experienced, and how he'd fallen asleep for hours on a big rock. Juan Jose's eyes became huge when Sammy told him about the bandidos and his narrow escape from them. Too embarrassed, Sammy skipped the part about wetting his pants, and told him about the things he heard from the preacher, and how when he decided to follow Jesus, the empty place in his heart filled up. They spoke for hours about the things Sammy had learned, and the more Sammy told him, the more questions Juan Jose asked.

"But what does it mean, Samuél? To make him El Señor of your life?"

It means I have to do what He says.

"All the time?"

"I think so, yes."

"But how does He tell you? In dreams or visions or does He speak directly to you?"

Sammy shrugged. "I don't know yet. Raul told me to pray about my mom today, and I did the entire time I worked in the field, but He hasn't answered me yet."

Juan Jose thought about it for a minute and held up a finger. "Maybe He has to think about what you said before He responds."

Sammy shrugged again. "Maybe. But I know how to find out." He reached behind him and pulled out the Bible.

"What is it?"

"A Bible. It was my dad's, and Juan Jose listen to this, he used to call it The. Word. Of. God."

"Hijole!" (Wow.)

"Should we see what it says?"

"Yes!"

Sammy put the book on his lap and let the pages fall open. He started reading from the top of the page.

"'For God so loved the world, He gave his one and only Son that whoever believes in Him shall never perish but have everlasting life. For

God did not send His Son into the world to condemn the world, but to save the world through Him.'"

"That's exactly what the preacher said, and it's what my dad tried to tell me before he died." Sammy handed the book to Juan Jose and stood up in his excitement. "Do you see what this means? My dad didn't really die because he lives in Heaven now. And I'll see him again because now I have eternal life too, and..." He stopped speaking and looked at his friend, and then towards his house. Finally, Sammy's gaze lingered over the lights in the small village below.

"What is it, Samuél?"

"I don't understand what happens to people who don't follow Jesus."

"What does The Book say?"

"I don't know. Let's see." He sat down again and started reading from where he stopped. "'Whoever believes in Him is not condemned, but whoever does not believe stands condemned already because he has not believed in the name of God's one and only son.'"

"What is the meaning of condemned?"

"Condemned? I'm not sure, but I don't think it's good. Wait—I have an idea! I'll be right back." He ran toward his house and climbed inside his bedroom window. He reappeared a few minutes later with another book in his hand.

"What is it?" Juan Jose asked when Sammy reached the tree.

"A dictionary," he said, trying to catch his breath. He thumbed through the pages until he found what he was looking for. "Oh no, listen to what it says. Condemn means to doom."

"Like, to die?"

Sammy nodded. "Or be punished. I think it means they won't get to have eternal life with God."

"Dios mio (My God)," Juan Jose whispered, his eyes going wild and round. "I must talk to this Jesus, Samuél. Are you sure He came to take away my sins, too?"

"Yes. The Bible says whoever believes in Him will have eternal life."

"But I've done some really bad things. Like the other day I snuck into Senora Hinojosa's henhouse and dyed all the eggs purple."

"Why?"

He shrugged. "I'm always doing bad stuff like that, Samuél. I guess I was just born that way."

"Well… what happened with the eggs?"

"She called the women of the village to boast about her special hens. I think she might have sold a few for a good profit. But it was still a bad thing to do, no?"

Sammy tried not to laugh out loud at the thought of his friend sneaking into the neighbor's hen house at night with purple dye. "Honestly, I think it's pretty funny, but I guess it wasn't exactly the right thing to do."

"Do you think Jesus will forgive me?"

"Well, the preacher said Jesus will forgive us of our sins if we ask Him."

"I want to. And I want to live with Him forever."

"And make Him the ruler over your life? The preacher said we can't just say the prayer and stay the same."

"I will proudly serve a man who died for the likes of someone like me."

"Okay, let's tell Him!"

The two boys knelt underneath the tree and prayed as its branches swayed in the breeze. Unseen to them were the thousands of angelic beings clapping and cheering them on, creating the wind that swirled around them.

Raul took extra care dressing for dinner. Mona was busy in the kitchen putting the final touches on their meal, and Raul decided to put on his best shirt for the occasion. He wanted to speak to her about the things he heard last night, but he expected resistance. Mona hadn't been open to talking about God for many years, but until now it hadn't mattered. They didn't share a faith, and God had never been a part of their lives. Raul had felt pulled in that direction a few times throughout the years, but every time he'd expressed his interest to Mona, she'd refused to consider it. He hoped tonight would be different now that he understood the importance of it all.

He walked out the bedroom with a hopeful determination. In the kitchen, Mona was busy setting out the dishes for their dinner. Raul took the drinking glasses out of her hands and placed them on the table.

"Gracias, esposo (husband)." She did a double take. "What is that you're wearing? Your best shirt?"

"What? I can't get dressed up for a dinner date with my best girl?"

Mona laughed and shook her head. "Raul, we haven't had a date in years. Now sit down, dinner's ready."

Raul sat down in the same chair he'd sat in for years, but for the first time in a long time, he felt nervous. He prayed silently that Mona would listen to what he had to say.

She brought two plates piled high with fried tostadas and all the fixings and sat one of them down in front of Raul. The hot oil glistened on the crisp tostadas, and Raul bent over the plate and inhaled the delicious scent. *There's nothing like the smell of freshly fried corn tortillas,* he thought. He glanced at Mona, and a small part of him wanted to postpone the conversation. It felt good to sit down to a simple dinner with his wife, but he shouldn't wait to talk to her. It was just too important. "Esposa (wife), there is something I want to talk to you about."

"What is it?"

Raul thoughtfully chewed a bite of his crunchy tostada while studying Mona. He loved her so much. She had worked hard over the years to make sure they were comfortable in their home, and she always made him feel appreciated. Mona didn't show her feelings the way some other women did, but he had never once doubted that she loved him. He tenderly reached out to take her hand. "I heard some things at the revival, and I'd like to tell you about them."

She nodded, and he went on. "You and I have only been to church a couple of times, and when we did go, we didn't hear anything that impacted us in any significant way."

Mona nodded in agreement.

"But things changed for me at the revival. The man who spoke talked about God as someone we can come to know intimately. And he spoke of God's sacrifice for us. I learned why Jesus had to hang on the cross, and now I feel so…" He took a sip of his water to quench the dryness overtaking his mouth. "Will you let me tell you what I learned?"

She shrugged. "I guess so."

So he did. He told her everything the preacher had spoken about at the revival, and how it had made him think about his life. He decided not to tell her that the preacher used to be friendly with Hector Mendez, or that he was the same man who had told the Juarazes about God so many years ago. Raul didn't want that to cause her to doubt the message. After he told her everything on his heart, he smiled. "I'm sorry I've gone on for so long. It's just that I feel so overwhelmingly grateful because of what I heard. I want to know this God, and I would like it very much if we could come to know Him together."

Mona drew in her breath. "Esposo, you know I've always been very cautious about these things."

"Yes, but maybe it's time to take a chance. Together."

She shook her head. "Raul, I am happy you have found something to give you peace, but please don't expect me to share it with you. I know you don't understand, but you will have to trust that I have my reasons."

He nodded and tried to smile, even as his heart broke. "Maybe in time," he said quietly.

"Sure, esposo. Maybe."

A loud, persistent knocking on the door pulled Sammy out of a deep satisfying sleep the next morning. He snuggled deeper under the covers, wishing his mom would hurry and answer the door so he could continue his dream.

But the knocking only became louder.

He peeked out of the covers, and to his surprise, discovered it was daylight. Why didn't his mom wake him up? He pushed aside his blanket and stood up, slid on his clothes and chose a pair of green Keds. The knocking had just started again when he pulled open the door.

"Raul! What are you doing here?" he asked, roughly rubbing the sleep from his eyes.

"I'm here to work, Samuél. And you? Why are you still in the bed?"

Sammy stepped back to let Raul inside. "My mom didn't wake me up. Where is she?"

"She is not here?"

Sammy shrugged. "Maybe she overslept. I'll go look." But when he looked into his mom's room, he saw she had already made her bed. She was nowhere in sight.

"Samuél, come here. I know where she is!"

Sammy followed Raul's voice to the kitchen where he saw his breakfast on the table and a small note in Raul's hand. "She said she had to go to town and will return in time for lunch."

Sammy plopped down in front of his cereal and poured in some milk. "That's weird."

"Yes." Raul poured the last of the coffee and sat next to Sammy.

"Juan Jose and I found something in the Bible last night," said Sammy in between bites of cereal.

"You have a Bible?"

Sammy nodded. "It said the people who don't call Jesus their Lord don't get to go to Heaven."

"Yes. It is true. I talked to Padre Salinas about it first thing this morning."

"Did he tell you where they went?"

"Yes."

Sammy waited with his spoon in mid-air. "Well?"

"It's not bueno, Samuél. The Padre say these people, they go to Hell."

"What's Hell?"

"The opposite of Heaven. It is a very bad place. And God is not there."

Sammy let this sink in. "Then why doesn't Padre Salinas preach to people about this place called Hell? I mean, if everyone knew they could choose between going to a good place or bad place when they died, why wouldn't they choose the good place?" He took a bite of cereal. "Raul, I don't think everyone knows. I sure didn't."

Raul sipped his coffee. "I do not think it is that simple."

"Why not?"

"Padre Salinas says that for some people, the belief does not come easy."

Sammy shook his head in frustration. "But if we explained things to them better maybe it would come easier."

Raul put down his coffee cup. "I tried Samuél. I tried very hard."

Sammy watched Raul wipe a tear from his eye and was surprised. He'd never seen him cry before. "Raul?"

"It is my Mona. She told me she does not want my Jesus."

Gabriella waited in her car, which had been sitting outside the bank since sunrise. She glanced at her watch again. The bank was due to open in ten minutes, which meant Hector Mendez would arrive at any moment. After so many years, she finally had a possible link to her parent's disappearance, and she needed to speak to the man to find out if he'd played a role in it. This would be a different conversation than ones they'd had in the past. When she had first arrived in town three years ago, she dealt with him when she opened an account at his bank. And since then, she'd seen him in town on many occasions, and they were always friendly and cordial with each other.

Gabriella was momentarily distracted by the people walking along the sidewalk. Most had their heads down, shoulders slumped and frowns across their faces. No one looked at anyone else—it was as if each person walked alone, shrouded in their own dim, private universe, too busy and apathetic to care about the other people around them. The scene left Gabriella with a hollowness, a feeling that the island—or rather life on the island—was slowly but steadily being eaten away by something. But she couldn't define what that something was.

A knock on the passenger car window startled Gabriella, and she turned to find Mona standing outside holding a large brown paper bag. She let her in.

When the door opened, a rush of stale air entered the car and was trapped inside when Mona slammed the door shut. "These are crazy days," she spurted. "First your son went to the revival without your permission, and now my husband…" She shook her head sadly. "He has lost his mind."

"Raul? What did he do?"

Mona waved her hand dismissively. "He wants me to be a church lady. You know, the kind of woman who bakes cakes, visits old people, and wears funny clothes."

Gabriella looked pointedly at Mona's outfit. Navy shirt with white stars plastered all over it paired with fluorescent floral pants. And again, the work boots. "So, he got religion?"

"Yes. With your son."

"The night of the revival?"

"Uh-huh." She nodded as she opened the bag and dug around in it. "But it is not a problem because I've done something to stop all this nonsense." She pulled out a handful of bright, colorful flyers.

"What are these?" Gabriella asked as she reached ne.

"Announcements for the village festival. It is two weeks from today."

"I don't understand. How will this help with Raul and Sammy?"

"Because at the meeting this morning, I signed them both up to volunteer with the festival. They have to pass out these flyers in the village starting tonight." She triumphantly held up the thin, colorful pieces of paper. "Between harvesting the grove and this, they will be too busy to think about the things of God."

Gabriella smiled and nodded. "That's a great idea. But Mona, you still haven't told me why you're so against God. What did He do to you?"

Mona pursed her lips and looked down. "It's not God I have a problem with. It's the people who claim to believe in him. I watched people I cared about very much be deceived by someone who called himself a man of God."

"What happened?"

She shook her head. "The time has not yet come to speak about this."

"But Raul, don't you see?" Sammy said. "There's no way Mona and my mom really understand. She thinks the only reason I want to know about God is because she was being a bad mom. But I don't think they understand what God is offering them, because if they did, they'd be as excited as we are."

Raul nodded. "So how to make them understand?"

Sammy shrugged. "What did Padre Salinas say?"

"He says some people just no like the religion."

Sammy spooned the last of the cereal into his mouth and then chewed it slowly, clearly troubled. "I know Padre Salinas understands a lot more about God and the Bible than I do, but it doesn't make sense to me that anyone in their right mind would turn down Heaven for Hell unless they don't believe they both exist."

Raul sat up straighter in his chair. "Yes, Samuél. I see what you mean."

"Wait here. I want to show you what Juan Jose and I found before he went home last night." Sammy scrambled outside to his favorite hiding place and returned with the Bible. He pushed his cereal bowel aside and sat down. "Listen to this. 'How then will they call on him in whom they have not believed? And how are they to believe in him of whom they have never heard? And how are they to hear without someone preaching?'" Sammy looked up. "We have to tell them, Raul. Or how else will they know?"

Raul took Sammy's hands in his and bowed his head. Sammy followed his lead and squeezed Raul's hands as he listened to the prayer. "Show us, Señor. Please show us what to do."

Gabriella looked up sharply when she heard a car door slam. "It's him."

"Hector Mendez? Is that why you are here?"

"Yes. I have some questions for him."

"About your parents?"

She nodded. "Raul told me some people believe he burned my parent's grove shortly before they disappeared."

"Yes, but no one knows for sure if Hector is the person who did it."

"I know that, but…" Gabriella sighed impatiently. "I can't take this not knowing anymore. I've been desperate to understand what happened to my parents for my entire life, and if Hector knows something, he needs to tell me. Between this and what's happening with Sammy, I feel like my life is spinning out of control." She sighed and softened her voice. "If I could only get control of a little piece of it…" She trailed off and looked at Mona with a renewed fire in her eyes. "It's time that I understand what happened to my parents." She pulled the handle and pushed against the door.

"Wait. I will come with you."

The pair walked briskly toward a meticulously dressed Hector, who hurried along the sidewalk.

"Señor Mendez."

He stopped and waited on the sidewalk for the two women to catch up. "Buenos dias Senoras. What can I do for you?" he asked in Spanish. His tone was friendly, but had an urgency to it, as if he had more important places to be.

Gabriella reached the man first. "My name is Gabriella, and I have an account at your bank."

"Of course," said Hector. "I hope everyone at the bank is treating you well?"

"Yes, but that's not why I'm here. You see, I set up an account under my married name, but I'm wondering if I should have used my maiden name. I lived here a long time ago, and I think some of the old-timers might better recognize me if I use my father's name."

Hector looked at her curiously. "Senora, if you want to change the name on your account, it's a simple matter. Just come inside with me, and I'll find someone to take care of the paperwork right away."

Gabriella shook her head. "I'm not making myself clear." She looked closely at Hector's eyes—she wanted to watch his reaction to what she was about to say. "The truth is, I want *you* to know my maiden name. Because I think you might have a questionable history with my family."

Mona moved closer to Gabriella in a show of support.

A look of impatience flashed across Hector's face, but he smiled and said, "Of course, Senora. And who is your family?"

"The Juarezes. Ring a bell?"

"Ignacio Juarez?"

"That's right."

"I don't understand. The Juarezes had a child?"

Gabriella didn't answer, but stared at him with her arms crossed in front of her.

Hector cleared his throat. "Well, I certainly knew Señor Juarez, but we weren't exactly what you would call close friends."

"No, I don't imagine a friend would have burned down his orange grove."

Hector's eyebrows shot up, and he turned to Mona in exasperation. "Will you please explain to this young lady that this village is full of people who have nothing better to do than spread false rumors?"

Mona shrugged.

Hector turned back to Gabriella. "Look, I'm very sorry about what happened to your parent's grove, but I can assure you I had nothing to do with it. And while it's true that your father and I did not see eye to eye on important matters, I would have never resorted to such tactics. Now, if you'll excuse me, I have to open the bank." He turned and walked away.

"What about their disappearance?" Gabriella called after him. "Did you have anything to with that?"

Hector continued to walk away, but threw up a hand and waved off the accusation.

"What do you think?" Mona asked as they watched him walk away.

"I think he knows a lot more than he's telling. And I won't stop until I know the truth."

After he entered the bank, Hector closed the door and leaned up against it. He wondered if it were true that the Juarezes had a child. *How could I not have known that? And if she really is their daughter, why has she reappeared after all these years?*

He walked to his office, closed the door and picked up the phone. It doesn't matter, he reassured himself. One curious woman couldn't undo everything they'd worked so hard to accomplish. He simply wouldn't allow it. He dialed the number he knew by heart. "It's me," he spoke into the receiver once the other person answered. "We have a problem."

Chapter 10

Later that afternoon, after Raul and Sammy put in a hard day's work in the grove, Mona and Gabriella broke the news to them that Mona had volunteered them to pass out the announcements in the village.

"What have you done?" Raul asked. "Don't you realize it's the harvest season? Where will we find time to do this as well?"

Mona shrugged. "I'm sorry, esposo. I thought you would be happy to help."

He looked closely at her and Gabriella. They were both on their knees scraping paint from the baluster posts along the front of the porch and seemed oblivious to the position they'd put him in. What were they up to?

"I made you guys some sandwiches you can eat on the way," Gabriella offered. "You know, to save you some time?"

"Yes," he said turning toward Sammy. "Let's get cleaned up, and then we will go."

Sammy raced inside, excited to be going into town with Raul. If he was lucky, Maria and her father would still be working their stand at the market. Maybe she'd give him an answer about rescheduling their date.

After a weary Raul and an excited Sammy drove off, sandwiches and announcements in hand, Mona turned to Gabriella. "Do you feel bad about what we did?"

Gabriella put down her tool, stood up and stretched. "A little. But then, we are in a battle, right? And personally, I'll do whatever it takes to win this one."

The village was just a short drive down the mountain from Sammy's house, and once they reached it, Raul decided it would be better if they split up. He dropped Sammy off at the south end of Rendiciòn near the market, intending to start at the north end to pass out his share of the flyers.

Sammy agreed to meet Raul at the Plaza after he'd passed out his flyers, and then he jumped out of the truck. As soon as his feet hit the ground, he headed straight to the market towards Maria, passing out flyers to apathetic villagers as he went.

Even though the sun was still high in the bright blue sky, the village appeared to be under a dark, heavy cloud. The people appeared to be just as dark, almost as if they were obscured by the shadow of the non-existent cloud. They trudged along the sidewalk in one slow moving grey mass, and Sammy felt a growing urge inside of him to tell them the good news he'd discovered.

When he reached the entrance to the market, he turned right and traveled down the row of make shift booths until he came to the one he was looking for. He found Maria towards the back of the booth, bent over and stacking the unsold produce into scarred wooden crates.

Immediately to his right, a vendor sold goat meat, and its distinctive aroma permeated the marketplace. A piñata maker occupied the booth across the way and he loudly told each passerby about his magnificent wares. To the left, a man stood stirring a large vat of grease, making chicharròns, as a hungry crowd gathered around and waited for the pig skin to finish frying.

"Hello, Maria," Sammy said shyly in Spanish. "I brought you an announcement for the village festival."

She straightened, a bushel of peppers in her hands, and stepped toward him. "Thank you, Samuél."

Sammy unconsciously stepped back, his mouth hanging open.

"What is it?"

He looked closer into his future wife's eyes. It wasn't there. The light was missing. *This can't be.* "Maria," he said, suddenly feeling bold. "We have to talk."

She nodded, looked over her shoulder for her father and then lowered her voice. "I know. I sent a message with Juan Jose this morning. Didn't you get it?"

He shook his head. "No, not about that. It's something much more important."

Her face collapsed into a combination of confusion and hurt. "More important than that?"

He nodded.

"Samuél, I'm beginning to think I'm making a big mistake by talking to you."

"I know it sounds strange," he said. "But you have to trust me when I say it's really important. When can I meet with you? To talk. Not for the other."

She looked hesitant. "I don't know…"

"I promise you this will be the most important conversation of your life."

She looked at him, obviously doubtful, but too curious to say no. "Bueno," she said." "Meet me at the cove tomorrow afternoon at four."

Raul stood on the corner offering flyers to everyone who passed by, but few took him up on the offer. He couldn't help but see the scowls on most people's faces. When did this happen, he wondered? *Have they always been this unhappy, and I've just never noticed it before? Is my newfound joy making me see things in a new light?*

He saw a familiar face in the crowd. "Estevan!" He called to him in Spanish. "I'm glad to see you, my friend. How are you?"

When the man saw Raul, he ambled over to him. "Raul, what are you doing here? I thought you would be busy in the grove. Isn't it harvest season?"

"Yes, but Mona volunteered me to pass out these flyers for the festival. Did you get one?"

"Gracias," he said, taking a flyer without even looking at it. "How is Mona?"

Lost, he thought. "She's good. And your family? How are they?"

"About the same. Just struggling to get by."

"I'm sorry, Estevan. I didn't realize your family was having problems."

"Problems? No, we don't have any problems."

Raul cocked his head. "I don't understand. I thought you said you were struggling."

"Yes, but not with any specific problems." He looked across the plaza, a look of desperation in his eyes. "You know, we're all just struggling with life. Trying to get by one day at a time."

Raul's heart ached for his friend. "That's not necessary, my friend."

"What do you mean?"

"I know someone who can replace your struggles with peace."

Sammy handed out as many announcements as he could at the market and then headed toward the pier. He was tortured by the lifeless eyes in the people he saw. Walking, but not truly alive. Empty, but not aware of it. In need of a Savior, but not knowing He exists.

He made his way to the pier, where a large gathering of people collected and sorted the fish caught that day. They would sell the best of the lot to the market vendors and stores, and the remainder would be sold in bulk. Sammy became hot and started sweating, and he wondered if he should have worn a lighter shirt. He turned his attention back to the crowd of people somberly working on their tasks around him, and suddenly a verse from the Bible popped into his head. "*How can they believe in the one in whom they have not heard? And how can they hear without someone preaching to them?*"

Yes, Sammy thought. Someone must tell them. If only they knew, perhaps the oppressive darkness would lift from the village. The heat inside of him intensified to the point where he had to dip his hand into a stray bucket of water and drip the cool liquid over his head. It didn't help. The fire burning inside of him magnified to an almost unbearable level, and he thought it would consume him if he couldn't figure out how to cool down.

And then it hit him.

"No, Lord. It can't be me." Panicked, Sammy looked around at the mostly grown men, along with a few teenagers and young guys. *They won't listen to me, God. I'm just a kid. I don't even know what to say.* But the flame wouldn't subside and instinctively Sammy understood there was only one way to make it stop.

Terrified, he picked up one of the abandoned wooden crates and carried it to the center of the activity. He turned the crate upside down, stood on it and cleared his throat. "Excuse me," he said in a small voice. "Um… excuse me?" But the bustle of activity continued around him. The crowd either couldn't hear him, or didn't care what a little kid had to say. Embarrassed, Sammy was about to climb down, when he thought about what Raul had told him in the grove. *We must pray, Samuél.* He took a deep breath and bowed his head.

"Jesus, I'm so scared. I can see these people need You, but I don't know how to tell them about You. Please help me. Amen."

He looked up. Nothing had changed, but he felt a new boldness that hadn't been there before. "Excuse me!" he said, startling even himself with the loudness and authoritative quality of his voice. Most of the men paused and looked up.

"I have something important to tell you, and I need your full attention. What I have to say is for those of you who have a restless heart. Maybe you're always looking for something around the corner, or maybe," he said looking each man into his listless eyes. "You've given up on the search, thinking that whatever you'd hoped for doesn't exist. I have good news for you! What your heart aches for does exist, but it's not something, it's someone, and his name is Jesus Christ."

Gabriella pulled the sweet-smelling orange spice cake from the oven and took a deep whiff. "Perfect," she declared.

"It's the least we could do after sending them off on such a mission," said Mona. "I am sure they will come home tired. Pobres."

"Yes," said Gabriella, pulling down two mugs from the cabinet for the freshly brewed coffee. "But it will keep them out of trouble, won't it?"

Raul and Estevan sat on a bench for a long time and talked about things, and by the time they finished, a new light shone in Estevan's eyes. "My friend," he told Raul. "I will be forever grateful to you for the things you have told me. And now, I must go and share this good news with my family."

After the two men said their goodbyes, Raul watched Estevan walk away, a new bounce in his step. *Lord, why can't it be that easy with my Mona?* He mentally compared what he'd told Mona and Estevan, and realized it was the same. So why hadn't Mona been able to see what Estevan did? The question weighed heavily on his mind.

He quickly passed out the remaining flyers and began walking to the plaza in search of Samuél. Once there, he scanned the area, but saw no sign of the boy. Raul watched as the sun begin its nightly slide into the sea and groaned. They would have to start work very early in the grove the next morning. He started up the road that led to the pier and asked people along the way if they'd seen Samuél. Finally, after a half-dozen no's, one man nodded and pointed to the pier.

Raul heard Samuél before he saw him. *Could that really be him?* The boy's voice was loud and confident and carried great authority.

"Yes, It's true that God loves us all," Sammy declared loudly. "And there's nothing you can do to make Him love you any more or any less. But," he said, stopping for emphasis. "The eternal life He offers us has conditions. He asks nothing more than for you to not only call him Lord, but treat him as Lord of your life as well. Jesus Himself asked, 'Why do you call Me Lord, Lord and not do what I tell you?'"

Raul rounded the corner and what he saw took his breath away. Men everywhere had abandoned their boats, their fish and their duties. They were crowded around Sammy, pressing inward and desperate for The Word. Some were at the back of the crowd on their knees with their heads already bowed and their lips moving. Raul saw light after light flicker on in the eyes of the crowd.

"If you want this joy, this peace, this everlasting life, bow to Him now and tell Him," Sammy continued. "He's waiting for you—can't you hear Him calling you? That tug on your heart, the lump in your throat, and that thirst in your mouth—it's Him. It's your Lord calling you! Will you answer Him?"

Raul leaned against an old rusted barrel. He was stunned. Awestruck. Scared. The preacher had been right—Samuél did have a calling on his life. But how would he answer it when his mom would fight him every step of the way? He made up his mind to find the preacher again. There were many things they had to discuss.

Sammy stepped down among the weeping, the praying and the spontaneous singing that had broken out among the men, and he moved away from the crowd. The fire was gone from within him, and had been replaced with a calmness, a feeling of having just woken up from a pleasant dream.

A man Sammy knew to be a bitter, angry old fisherman reached out and hugged him. "Dios te bendiga, hijo."

"God bless you too, sir."

What happened, Lord? Where did those words come from? He looked at the men who'd listened to him speak and was surprised to see some of them were still kneeling with their hands lifted to the sky. *Lord, You are amazing!* Sammy watched with wonder as the men's eyes, which had been so grave and hopeless before, now shone with the truth. But wait, some of the men's eyes were hard and unchanged. Why? How could anyone reject the One who loved them so?

It was getting dark and Sammy realized that Raul would be getting worried, so he headed out in the direction of the Plaza.

"Samuél."

Sammy turned toward the soft voice and saw Raul. He ran to him and threw his arms around his waist. "Raul! I don't know what happened. The words started coming and I couldn't stop speaking them. How did I even know all that stuff about God?"

"I saw you," Raul whispered, hugging the boy close. "God used you,

Samuél. It is the truth. He must have spoken through you." He pulled away and looked more closely at him. "God has a plan for your life just like the preacher said." He pulled Sammy close again. "But how to tell your mother?"

Chapter 11

Sammy walked sleepily into the kitchen the next morning and sat down at the table. "Good morning Mom. Can I have another piece of orange spice cake for breakfast?"

Gabriella shut the refrigerator door and paused to kiss the top of Sammy's head on the way to the stove. "Not for breakfast, but you can have a piece after lunch. Your eggs are almost ready."

"Yes, ma'am." He poured a glass of milk and gulped it down. "Are you helping us in the grove again today?"

"No, I'm going to try and finish scraping the posts on the porch so Mona and I can get started painting tomorrow."

He nodded. "Mom?"

"Hmm?" She set a plate of eggs in front of him and then sat in the chair next to his.

"I..." Sammy sighed in frustration. Why did the words come so easily last night in front of a bunch of strangers, but wouldn't come for the most important person in his life? He'd stayed up late reading his dad's Bible last night, and he found the parts about Hell. Raul was right—it wasn't a good place, and he didn't want his mom to go there. *Lord, give me the words*, he prayed silently. "Mom? Do you know about Hell?"

He watched her lips tighten and then force themselves into a smile. "Yes, Sammy. I've heard the stories."

"But do you believe it's real?"

"Of course not. Now eat your breakfast, it's going to get cold."

"Yes ma'am." He smeared butter on a triangle of toast and shoved half of it into his mouth. He chewed it thoughtfully. "But why?"

"Why would you want to eat it cold?"

"No," he shook his head. "Why don't you think Hell is real? Jesus did."

She sighed. "Look Sammy, if there was a God, and I'm not saying there is, do you really think He'd want his creation to burn in some horrible fire forever?"

"No ma'am."

"You see? That's why I don't believe Hell exists. Now eat your eggs."

"But that's why He sent Jesus."

"Excuse me?"

"The reason Jesus came was to take away our sins so we don't have to go to Hell."

She patted his hand. "I'm sorry, Sammy. As nice as those stories sound, they're really just made up by people who are desperate to make sense of their lives."

"Do you believe in the Bible?"

"No."

He scrunched up his face in puzzlement. "So you think all those people just guessed those things would happen before they did? And they got lucky?" He put down his fork. "Every. Single. Time?"

"Sammy, you have a long morning ahead of you in the grove, and you need some nourishment. Please?"

He picked up his fork and took a bite, then, "Mom?"

"Yes, Sammy," The impatience sounding in her voice.

"What if you're wrong?"

Sammy didn't mean to make his mom upset, but he did. She'd become brisk in her movements and stopped talking after he asked her what would happen if she was wrong about the Bible. Sammy couldn't understand why she didn't see what was so clear. So, it was with a downcast spirit that he answered the door a few minutes later.

"Hi Raul. What are you doing here, Juan Jose?"

"I'm off of restriction," his friend announced happily. "Raul stopped by this morning to do some work on the chicken coop, and he asked my mom if I could come and help in the grove. Esta bueno, no?"

"Yeah, it's good. Wait for me while I put on my shoes, okay?"

Raul and Juan Jose looked at each other, puzzled by Sammy's mood. "What's wrong, Samuél?" Juan Jose asked. "You look very sad."

Sammy glanced toward the kitchen where his mom was still cleaning up the breakfast dishes. "I don't know. Nothing's going like I thought it would."

"What is this all about?" Raul asked, putting his hand on Sammy's shoulder. "After last night, I thought you would be very happy."

Tears formed in the corners of Sammy's eyes, but he wiped them away before they could fall. "Let's go outside," he said brusquely.

When they reached the grove, all three of them sat on the end of the sagging trailer. The sweet-smelling aroma of ripening oranges hung heavily in the air, reminding Sammy of how bitter things really were. "I don't get it," Sammy said. "Why are my mom and Mona so stubborn? And why don't they want to go to Heaven? I don't understand why total strangers will listen to me, but not the people closest to me?"

"I listened to you," said Juan Jose. "And now I no longer have the hole in my heart."

"I don't know why some people will listen the truth and others won't," said Raul. "But we can find out tonight."

"What do you mean? How?"

"The preacher agreed to meet us in town tonight after we pass out the rest of the flyers. I told him we have many questions."

"There's more," Sammy whispered to Juan Jose after Raul climbed down and headed off to work.

"What is it?"

"Maria."

"Si Samuél! I forgot to tell you! I talked to her, and—"

"—I know. I saw her last night. But it's not about the date."

His eyes opened wide. "What else is there?"

Sammy took a deep breath. "Juan Jose, you know I want to marry her."

"Yes…"

"But I can't. And if I can't marry her, it would be wrong for me to hold her hand."

"Not hold her hand?" Juan Jose stared at him dumbfounded. "But we worked so hard. I don't understand."

"Look what I found last night in my dad's Bible." He reached into his pocket, pulled out a piece of paper and began to read. "'Do not be unequally yoked with unbelievers.' At first, I didn't understand what the word yoked meant, so I looked it up in the dictionary."

"And?"

"It means joined together. Don't you see? I can't hold Maria's hand unless she becomes a believer in Jesus!"

"Hijole."

After lunch on the porch which included generous slices of the orange spice cake, Raul announced that it was time to get back to work. Sammy and Juan Jose did their best to stall by negotiating for more of the cake, and Gabriella finally relented and agreed that after the afternoon's work, they could each have another slice. Shortly after that, Gabriella watched as Raul and the two boys headed back to the grove. She picked up the paint scraper but immediately put it back down. She felt restless. Like she was being called by something—or someone. Sammy's unbending belief in God and the Bible had unsettled her. And while she admired her son for having such strong opinions, she knew it was dangerous. Why couldn't he feel that strongly about something innocuous like sports or girls? The wind tugged at her, and she soon found herself wandering near the cliff.

She stayed back, didn't go to the edge of the cliff this time and instead stared out at the unsettled sea. The disorderly wind was beating the waves, driving them this way and that until they were nothing more than a mass of churning, directionless waters.

Why do I feel so restless?

Sammy changed clothes half a dozen times in preparation for the date with Maria. *It's not a date*, he reminded himself. *But still, it wouldn't hurt a guy to look good, would it?* He finally settled on his nicest pair of jeans, a green T-shirt and his orange Keds. The orange ones always made him feel brave.

Earlier in the grove, he'd broken down and told Raul everything that had been happening with Maria. Raul agreed that it wouldn't be right to hold her hand under the circumstances and then added that he was too young to be thinking about marriage anyway. *Not that it matters now*, Sammy thought glumly.

He put his dad's Bible in his backpack and slung the bag over his shoulder. He headed to his bedroom door, but stopped before he reached it. *What am I forgetting?* When he finally realized what it was, he knelt down and called out to the one who could open Maria's ears to the truth.

After working in the grove, Raul decided to take a short nap before going to town and finishing with the flyers. He'd been tired lately, and the ache in his chest seemed to be getting stronger. *A good nap will do me some good*, he thought.

When he walked into the bedroom, he was disappointed to find that Mona had stripped off the linens from the bed to wash them. She wasn't back from running her errands, and Raul felt too tired to do it himself. Not wanting to delay his nap, he wandered into the guest bedroom to lie down.

He gratefully lowered his aching body onto the sagging bed and closed his eyes. But no matter how hard he tried, he couldn't get comfortable. Frustrated, Raul got up to fluff the old down bed. But when he picked up the mattress, he saw the source of his discomfort. In the middle of the drooping box springs sat an old carved wooden box.

What's this? He removed the box and repositioned the feather bed. Sitting down, Raul slid back the wooden lid and was surprised to find a single piece of paper inside the box. Puzzled, he took it out and began to read it. And then wished he hadn't.

"My God," he mumbled. "This changes everything."

Sammy sat on the biggest rock he could find at the cove and watched the water run in bravely over the sand, only to retreat in shimming fear just as quickly. He looked at his dad's watch for the hundredth time since he'd arrived. 4:22. Maybe Maria wasn't coming.

"Hola, Samuél."

He looked up to see the prettiest girl in the world walking toward him. She wore emerald green shorts and a poufy white blouse. Her hair, held back with a wide, green ribbon, hung past her shoulders and shimmered in the sun. She wore pink plastic sunglasses shaped like stars.

"Hello, Maria."

When she reached the rock, she sat down on the other side of it. "I'm here," she said. "What is it you want to talk to me about?"

Sammy cleared his throat and tried to find the words. What if she didn't listen? How would he live without her as his wife?

"Well?" she asked. Even though she sat facing the sea, Sammy thought he saw a slight smile cross her lips.

"Maria, something's happened to me."

"Yes, I know. I heard what happened last night at the plaza."

Sammy felt his face turn red. "You did?"

"Yes."

"Oh. Well…" He shrugged. "Then I guess you already know." He paused, horrified that he couldn't find a way to form a coherent sentence. "So, how did you hear?"

"My father was there."

Sammy gulped. "Your… your father heard me speak?"

She nodded.

Sammy groaned softly. If her father, who had never really warmed to him anyway, heard him speak last night, he must have told Maria what a fool he'd made of himself. How he, a mere boy, had tried to tell grown men what to do with their lives. But men's lives *had* been changed, he reasoned with himself. How could he possibly make her understand that?

The silence between them dragged on and little beads of perspiration began to form on Sammy's upper lip. He wanted to slink away, to disappear and never have to face Maria again.

"He told me to thank you," she finally said.

"Huh? Why would he thank me?"

"Because," she said, turning toward him. "You have given our family that which we haven't known before."

"Maria! You…. you…"

"Yes Samuél," she said, laughing. "My father shared the good news with my family. So you see, I already know the news you came to tell me about."

Sammy beamed. "Will you do me a favor?"

"Of course."

"Take off your sunglasses."

"My sunglasses?"

"Humor me, okay?"

She smiled shyly, then reached up and pulled them off. "Is that better?" Her eyes shone with the light that comes from the knowledge of the truth.

"You believe," he whispered. Before he could think about what he was doing, he scooted across the rock and hugged her. "Now there's nothing to keep me from marrying you!"

"Marrying me?"

Shocked at what he'd just said, Sammy suddenly pulled away and repositioned himself back on his side of the rock. He felt the heat rise in his face and knew that it was deep red. The tips of his ears burned fiercely.

"Holding your hand," he mumbled. "I meant there's nothing keeping me from doing that."

She nodded, trying unsuccessfully to restrain a giggle. "Well?"

"Well, what?" he asked, still trying to recover.

"Do you want to hold my hand or not?"

Sammy felt his face flush again. Could this day get any better, he wondered? "Sure. Okay. I mean… yeah. I do."

"Do you remember the rules?"

"Uh-huh."

"Okay then." She turned away from him and slid her hand across the rock until it reached the halfway point. "Remember, you can't tell anyone," she said.

Sammy hesitated. "Not even Juan Jose? He's my best friend and we tell each other everything."

She considered this for a moment, then "Okay, but only him."

Sammy took a deep breath and reached for her hand. They were faced away from each other, and when Sammy's hand touched hers, he breathed out a sigh of relief. He only hoped she couldn't hear his heart pounding against his chest. It wasn't long before both of their hands were wet with perspiration, but neither of them pulled away. They sat that way for what seemed like hours.

"Do you really want to marry me?" she asked, breaking the silence.

Sammy sighed contently. "More than anything."

"Okay," she said. "I have to go now and help my father in the market."

"Yes, of course," he said, suddenly embarrassed again.

Maria hopped off the rock and started down the beach toward the market. As Sammy watched her go, he had an overpowering urge to do something heroic, something that would seal this moment in both of their minds forever.

"Maria," he called after her impulsively.

She turned around and put her hand on her hip. "Yes, Samuél?"

"I, uh…" he smiled his crooked grin, stuck for words again. "I mean… uh…"

"I know," she said, her giggles mixing and dancing with the wind. "Me, too."

Later that night as Raul passed out the festival announcements in town, he noticed a large man lumbering toward him. He studied Preacher as he neared, aware that since reading the letter, he felt the need to be cautious around him. "Preacher," he said as the man approached.

"Raul." He thrust his hand forward to shake Raul's. "Where's the boy?"

Raul nodded his head toward the wharf. "I will take you to him and let you see for yourself."

"Okay then, let's go."

As they neared the wharf, Sammy's voice mingled with the wind and raced toward them. "What are you waiting for men?" Sammy asked loudly. "Do you truly believe you're going to find yourselves a better deal than the one God Almighty is offering you? Are you so misled you think the fleeting pleasures of this short life are worth sacrificing an eternity in paradise for? Let me ask you a question: who do you think authored the lie that the things of this world are better than the things of the next?"

As Raul and Preacher rounded the corner, they saw the crowd gathered around Sammy. Many of them knelt down, crying out to the One who could save them. Sammy stood on the old upturned crate, hands raised to the heavens, eyes closed. He continued to speak.

"Don't let Satan steal your soul, which will live forever. He wants you to share in his darkness and torment, and he will do everything he can to trick you into believing that this life is the only one that matters. But it's not, and there is One who is whispering your name even as I speak, urging you to make Him your King so you can live forever with Him in glory."

Preacher turned to Raul. "What's this?"

Raul shrugged. "I'm not sure. Samuél says a fire burns within him whenever he gets around a crowd, and it's so strong that speaking the Word of God is the only way he can relieve it."

"How long has this been going on?"

"This is the second night he has spoken."

Preacher nodded and turned his attention back to the boy on the crate. He shook his head slowly, never taking his eyes off Sammy. "Well, I'll be."

Mona came to a skidding halt in front of the yellow house and shoved open the car door. The air was changed with concern as she thudded up the wooden steps and banged on the door. "Gabriella! Come! Be quick!"

She raised her hand to knock again when the door flew open.

"Mona, what is it?" Gabriella asked.

Mona grabbed her arm and tried to pull her out to the porch. "Let's go!"

"Wait," said Gabriella, fear overtaking her slight features. "What's wrong? Is it Sammy?"

"Yes. It is your son," she said, continuing to pull her out the door.

"No," she sobbed. "Oh please, not again."

Mona realized what Gabriella must be thinking. "No… Samuél, he is okay."

"Then what? Mona, please. Tell me what's happened."

She forced herself to slow down and look at Gabriella. Mona pitied her for what she was about to hear because she understood how deeply it would hurt her. "Samuél," she whispered. "He is preaching to the men in the village."

Gabriella stepped back as if pushed by the wind. "He's… preaching?"

"Yes. And the men, they listen to him."

"How do you know? Did you see him?"

Mona shook her head. "No, I did not see him. But Senora Herrera told me her husband listened to Samuél preach last night, and he is going back tonight to hear more."

"This can't be," Gabriella said, tears filling her eyes. "How does Sammy know enough to preach?"

Mona shrugged. "You want that I should take you?"

Gabriella stood up straight, a fierce determination spreading over her delicate features. "Yes," she said. "It's time I end this once and for all."

Mona saw the swollen clouds seconds before the rain began lighting tapping on the porch roof. She reached inside and pulled out Gabriella's raincoat from the hook. "It is best if we take this," she said. "The storm. It is coming now."

Once Sammy exhausted himself, he stepped down and slowly found his way to Raul and Preacher. He was filled with embarrassment when he saw Preacher and shyly moved toward Raul.

"Good to see you again, son."

"Yes sir," he said, cautiously holding out his hand to shake the preacher's.

"I see God is already working in your life."

Sammy shrugged.

"Samuél," Raul said. "What is wrong with you?"

He shrugged again. "I can't help it," he said in a small voice, a huge contrast from the booming one they'd heard only minutes before.

"Your preaching?"

He nodded. "Yes, sir."

Preacher knelt down, difficult for a man of his size, and looked directly at Sammy. "Son, you have nothing to be ashamed of. It's God Himself who is putting those words in your mouth."

"But I'm just a kid. It doesn't seem right for me to be talking to grown men like that."

"Have you tried to stop?"

Sammy looked down at his neon yellow Keds. "Yes, sir."

"And what happened?"

"The fire in me gets hotter and hotter until I can't stand it anymore, and I have to say those things to feel better."

Preacher turned his gaze toward the crowd, some of whom were still on their knees weeping before the Lord. "Shut up in my bones," he said under his breath. He pointed toward the crowd. "Look at them, Sammy. What do you see?"

He scanned the crowd. "Light," he whispered. "I see light in places where there was darkness before."

Preacher nodded. "The Lord will use these very stones to cry out to these men if He has to, but He has chosen you." He put his hand on Sammy's shoulder. "It's a great and terrifying thing to be chosen by the Lord, son. But it's no use fighting it. Do you understand me?"

Sammy looked again at the crowd and saw in a flash how the lives of these men would change because of God's words. He thought of Maria, and how her entire family had been affected because her father heard the Truth. Then he understood with clarity that he had a role, a mission for God's Kingdom that had been carefully designed and mapped out before the beginning of time. He wondered if his dad was there, in Heaven, listening to him preach, clapping his hands and urging him on in his role.

Finally, with a Rock solid determination, he turned his gaze back to Preacher. "Yes sir," he said solemnly. The first drops of a new rain began to fall on his face. "I believe I do."

Mona flew down the muddy road leading to the village, and the windshield wipers worked furiously to keep the now driving rain at bay. Gabriella sat in the passenger seat. She desperately tried to fight the devastating memories of her past, but they were coming with hurricane force. The time she was five and had been awakened by loud noises. Her parents driving away in the dead of the night, and her questioning why they would leave without her, but believing in her naïve heart they would return. And then slowly, over the next couple of days, realizing they might not come back for her after all. And then she remembered the unfamiliar woman who had come to the house one night. When the woman found Gabriela hiding in her parent's closet, she had spoken to her in soft, comforting tones, but Gabriella had been inconsolable. It was as if she knew, even as a young girl, her life would never be the same. The woman picked her up and carried her away, never bothering to explain to her that she would never see her parents again.

Next, an image of her aunt flashed in her mind. She remembered how her mother's sister, who had immigrated to South Texas, had grudgingly taken her in. Before she fully understood what was happening, Gabriella had found herself in a world full of people who spoke a language she didn't understand, foods she didn't like, and a sense of being out of place and a bother to everyone she needed. And then her aunt had died, selfishly taking with her the secrets Gabriella was so desperate for.

And then there were Nicolas's parents. They had brought her into their fold so easily, with such warmth and love, satisfying her overwhelming desire to be loved again. But they'd been snatched away from her so suddenly, so cruelly on that dark and stormy night. A night not so different from this one.

Next, Gabriella felt the haunting presence of Nicolas, her love, the man she trusted with her entire heart. He had left her, too. All of them were snatched away ruthlessly by the tyrant in the sky, and now He had Sammy in his grasp, luring him in, making him believe He was safe, secure. He would cause Sammy to let down his guard, trust in the untrustworthy, and believe in His lie. And then it would come. The one thing that was unthinkable, the thing she simply couldn't survive. He would take her son from her, too.

"Hurry Mona," she whispered. "I've got to reach Sammy before it's too late."

Chapter 12

Raul, Sammy and Preacher ducked into a fonda, a small family restaurant, to get out of the increasingly hard rain.

"What now?" Preacher asked as he watched the rain come down in slanted sheets.

"Let's get a table," said Raul. "We have some things to discuss."

They settled at a table pushed into the corner of the room, one generally used for private conversations that had the potential to alter the course of someone's life. "I'm starving," said Sammy. "Can we eat?"

They called over the waitress and placed their order, convincing Sammy to eat a meal before the tres leches cake he had his eyes on. They tried to make small talk until their food arrived, but it proved difficult because Raul was lost in his thoughts. He desperately needed to ask Preacher about the letter but didn't want to bring it up in front of Samuél. Finally, the waitress arrived with hot metal plates overflowing with chicken enchiladas topped with cream, perfectly prepared rice and charred pinto beans. They piled on lettuce and tomatoes from the bowls sitting in the center of the table and then set about the task of obliterating all traces of food from their plates. Sammy got his cake, and afterwards, they all leaned back from the table, giving their stomachs some extra room to breathe.

"I have a question," Sammy said. "Why do some people want to go to Heaven, but others don't?"

"Because," sighed Preacher. "Some people think they can run their lives better than the Lord can."

"Huh?"

He leaned his portly body forward, pushing aside his empty plate. "The way I see it," he said, "is that there are four kinds of people when it comes to God. The first kind is like you and Raul. They recognize the incredible gift God is offering and grab hold of it like a lifeline. Others are so confident in themselves their pride won't allow them to admit their need for anyone else. The third kind is living a life that isn't pleasing to God, and to recognize Him as Lord would mean they would have to turn from sin. And they don't want to do that." He took a sip of his coffee and sighed. "And then there are the others. The hurt ones."

"The hurt ones?"

"Hmm. The people who have been so beat up by life they turn against God instead of toward Him for comfort."

"But why?"

He shrugged. "It's easier, I guess, to have someone to blame when things don't go as we think they should. You see, if they put all their energy and emotions into blaming Him, they never really have to face their pain.

"What they don't realize is that the Bible tells us to cast our cares upon Him because He loves us. But when someone's been horribly hurt, it can be difficult to trust Him. You see, until someone like this comes to the end of themselves and their own abilities, they have no capacity to see God. And how do you realize you need someone who you don't even know is there?"

Sammy nodded, thinking about his mom and Mona. And he suddenly understood a whole lot more. He leaned forward and said in an urgent voice, "Tell me, Preacher. I need to know what it takes to reach the hurt ones."

Mona slammed into the rubber barriers at the dock, unable to stop the car from skidding on the slick pavement. Before they came to a complete stop, Gabriella flung open her door, got out and fought the driving rain. "Sammy!" she cried into the combative wind. "Sammy, where are you?"

Mona appeared next to her, wrapping a raincoat around her shoulders. "He is not here!" she yelled, trying to be heard above the storm. "Let's go back to the car."

Gabriella shook her head, her long wet hair flinging water in every direction. "I'm not leaving without my son." But as she looked around the deserted wharf, she realized Mona was right. Sammy had been here, she was sure, but now he was gone. "They must have taken shelter someplace," she said, sliding into the slick passenger seat. "Let's go into town and try and find him there."

"Love and prayer," Preacher said in answer to Sammy's question. "That's the only way to show the hurt ones they can trust God."

"I don't understand."

"Think of it this way. If you thought your best friend had done something to hurt you, how would you feel?"

Sammy pushed the damp curls off his forehead and thought about how he would feel if Juan Jose did something bad to him. "I would be really upset," he said. "I might even try to avoid him. I sure wouldn't trust him again that's for sure."

"Okay. Now what would it take for you to be able to trust him again? Be his friend again?"

Sammy shrugged. "I don't know. I guess he'd have to prove he didn't really mean to hurt me. And that he wouldn't do it again."

"What if you found out that what you thought he had done to hurt you was meant for your good? That you just didn't understand his actions?" When he saw the confused look on Sammy's face, he continued. "Think of it this way. What if Juan Jose made you walk the long way to school when you were tired, and you were upset with him because you thought he was just being mean. But later in the day, you learned there had been a pack of wild dogs near the shortcut, and he knew it. Would you still be mad?"

"No, I'd be glad he was looking out for me."

"It's the same with the hurt ones, son. They need to know they're loved by God, and the bad things they've experienced in their lives served a purpose, even though they may not understand that purpose this side of Heaven. They have to grasp this before they can trust Him."

"And what will make them understand?"

"We have a part in that."

"We do?"

"That's right, Sammy. First, we're to pray for them, and then be the hands, feet, eyes, ears and mouth of Jesus. He counts on us to show His love to the hurt ones."

"They're not in there!" Gabriella yelled, coming out of the small store.

"Maybe they went home," Mona said, trying to shelter herself from the storm underneath a tattered awning. "You want I should take you there?"

"Not yet," she answered, walking deliberately toward a small fonda. "Not until I've searched every place in the village."

Raul leaned forward, resting his elbows on the table. "Samuél, why don't you go to the restroom before we make the drive home?"

Sammy nodded, pushed back his chair and bounded toward the restroom. Raul turned his attention toward Preacher. "I remember you," he said.

Preacher cocked his head to one side in confusion. "Remember me? From the revival? Of course you do."

Raul shook his head. "No, from before. I remember you from many years ago when the tankers tried to dock here. But I haven't seen you since."

Preacher shook his head. "No, you wouldn't have. I've been traveling since then preaching the Word. I only occasionally pass through Rendiciòn now. But you do look a little familiar to me. How do we know each other?"

"I worked for a family then," continued Raul, not taking his gaze off of Preacher. "And you came to tell them about Jesus. In fact, I saw you visit them right before they disappeared."

Preacher's eyes widened. "Which family is that? And why did they disappear?"

"It's Samuél's family, the Juarezes. And no one knows why they disappeared."

Preacher leaned back heavily in his chair. "Yes, I remember the Juarezes well. But how is Sammy related to them?"

"He is their grandson."

"Well, I'll be." He sat in thought for a moment, and then, "I remember their little girl. Sammy is her son?"

Raul nodded, and then looked expectantly at Preacher, who had closed his eyes and become still. The storm outside was pounding on the large front windowpane, trying desperately to get inside.

"The boy's mother," Raul began, uncomfortable with the silence. "She's still trying to figure out what happened to her parents."

Preacher opened his eyes. "They were never found?"

"No."

Preacher leaned forward, bringing down the two front legs of his chair with a thud. Lightning flashed and the silhouette of a drenched woman running toward the restaurant appeared.

"And there's this," Raul said, reaching into his pocket and pulling out the frayed and yellowed piece of paper he'd found in the box. "I've been trying to make sense of it all day." He slid it across the table, his hand lingering over it as if he were afraid to let it go.

"May I?"

Raul nodded and reluctantly pulled back his hand.

Preacher pulled the delicate piece of paper toward him, and Raul watched as his features went from curious to troubled, and then settled on outrage. "Where did you get this?" he demanded.

"My wife has kept it hidden all these years."

"I don't understand why she would have done that."

Raul shrugged. "I found it hidden in our house." He leaned halfway across the table. "What I need to know Preacher, is why you left this note for the Juarezes."

Preacher's meaty hand hovered over the letter. He opened his mouth to speak several times, but each time, he sighed in frustration instead. Finally, he started to speak, but was interrupted by a commotion at the front of the restaurant.

The storm entered three steps ahead of Gabriella. Lightning flashed and the light bulbs flickered. The fierce downpour quickly drowned out all conversation at the scattered checkered-cloth tables, and all heads turned toward her.

She scanned the sparse crowd until her gaze landed on Raul and the strange looking heavy set man sitting across from him. "Raul!" she cried out. "Where is Sammy?" She made her way towards the men.

"He is in the restroom. Gabriella, what are you doing out here in this storm?"

She glowered at the men as the rain wept off her hair, hands, and the edge of her coat. "Is it true?" she sputtered. "Has Sammy been preaching at the wharf?"

"You're his mother?" Preacher boomed. "Do you realize the call God has put on that young man's life?"

She turned to face him. "And you are?"

"Now Gabriella," Raul started, but she held up her hand to silence him, never taking her eyes off Preacher. "Are you the reason for my son's disobedience?"

"Disobedience to whom?"

"To me, of course. I'm his mother."

"I'm afraid that he has a higher authority than you, ma'am."

"What?" She turned to Raul. "Who is this man?"

"He's the preacher, mom," a small voice said from behind her. "The one from the revival."

They all turned to find Sammy, his lopsided grin hopeful, his curls tamed with sink water. The sky groaned with the weight of the rain.

"Sammy! I've been worried sick about you. I heard you've been preaching to the men at the wharf."

He hung his head. "Yes ma'am."

Her jaw dropped. "Yes? Oh Sammy, how could you? Don't you understand? It's not real, son. You've been tricked." She turned toward

105

Preacher. "And you. How dare you instruct my son to go against my wishes?"

"It's not his fault," came Sammy's soft voice again. "I have to say the words God gives me, or my insides will burn up."

"That's enough," she said, grabbing hold of Sammy's hand and pulling him toward the door. "I won't listen to any more of this nonsense."

The wind pushed open the door and a soaked Mona entered the restaurant. She leaned against the doorpost and emptied the water from one of her boots and then the other. Mona searched the restaurant for the group, and when she found them, she tromped across the room towards them, leaving a small rivulet in her wake. "You found them," she said to Gabriella once she was at the table. "Is it true Raul?" "You allowed Samuél to preach?"

"Hold it everyone," said Preacher, his massive form rising out of the chair. "Let's all calm down and try to make some sense of this."

"That would imply you have a say-so in my son's life," Gabriella said, tugging on Sammy's sleeve. "Which you don't. Come on Sammy. We're going home."

"Wait. I think you should listen to him, mom."

She spun around to face Sammy, her eyes ablaze. "Sammy, this isn't open for discussion. I'm your mother, and you have to trust that I know what's best for you. I forbid you to pursue this God thing any further."

Sammy could barely make out his mom's face because of the tears pooling in his eyes, but he saw enough to confirm that her eyes were devoid of light. "I'm sorry, mom, but I can't. Even if I tried to stop, I wouldn't be able to."

She shook her head in frustration and pulled him toward the door.

Mona turned an anguished face toward Raul. Her already scrunched up features were balled tightly together. "How could you, esposo?" she asked. "I've never been ashamed of you until now. How could you go against Gabriella's wishes for her own son? Don't you understand how painful all of this is for her? And now you have made it worse."

Raul looked down and spread out his hands. "I don't know what to say. There is so much you don't understand."

"It's not his fault," said Preacher. "The boy was only obeying God's instructions."

Mona turned to face the portly man, and Raul saw a glimmer of recognition in her eyes. "What is your name?"

"They call me Preacher."

Mona gasped and took a step backwards. She reached out her hand to Raul and looked in disbelief at Preacher. "You're the man responsible for the Juarez's disappearance. She turned toward Raul. "Esposo, this man is not who he pretends to be."

"I found the letter, Mona. Preacher was just about to explain it."

She shook her head. "I don't understand. How can you join up with a man like this? Especially after reading that letter? Raul, think about what it could mean!"

"I'd like to give him the opportunity to explain."

"We'll talk about this later." She moved toward the door, and when Raul stood up to follow her, Preacher put his hand out to stop him.

"I feel an urgent need to pray," he said. "And I don't think it can wait."

Mona walked out of the restaurant and the wind instantly pushed against her, urging her back inside. But she fought against it, making her way toward Gabriella and Samuèl, who were already waiting in the car. She opened the door, struggled with it against the wind, and climbed inside. She pulled the door shut.

"Dios mio," she said. "This storm's a killer."

The sound of Sammy's sobs filled the car, and that combined with Gabriella's loud sighs told Mona words had been exchanged between them before she got in. "Bueno," she said. "We should all try and calm down."

"Calm down?" said Gabriella. "How can I do that? My son refuses to obey me, my foreman sneaks behind my back allowing my son to preach, and this... this God," she spat out the word. "He won't leave me be." She turned toward the back of the car to face Sammy. "Sammy, don't you understand? This God of yours, he's dangerous. He's come for you, just like he came for your dad, and he'll take you away from me, too. Please Sammy," she cried. "Please resist him."

"I…" Sammy choked back his tears. "I can't mom, but you're wrong about Him. Please let me try and explain."

Frustrated, Gabriella turned toward the front of the car. "Please drive us home, Mona." The tension ballooned to the breaking point as Mona pointed the car south and headed toward the yellow house on the cliff.

Preacher looked up at the same time as Raul. "Do you sense it?" he asked.

"Mucho peligro," Raul whispered urgently. "There is much danger."

They simultaneously shoved away their chairs and headed for the door. "I hope we're not too late," Preacher said as he opened the door and felt the wind and rain rush against him. "Jesus, please don't let us be too late."

Mona swerved the car in time to miss a pothole that was rapidly filling with storm water and then brought the car to a halt in front of the house. It appeared as if the heavens had opened up and were pounding away at the cliff with all their fury. Water slid down and cascaded off the roof so hard there was a solid wall of water they'd have to walk through just to get inside. The sea's ferocity could be felt, and it threatened to engulf them and everything around it.

Gabriella, who had been quiet the entire ride home, shoved against the door and allowed the rain to crash into the car. Without a word, she stepped outside and was immediately engulfed in the storm. She walked, seemingly in no hurry, through the battering rain and up the steps before letting herself into the house.

Sammy sniffed. "Are you mad at me, too?"

Mona let out a long sigh and turned around to face him. "Samuél," she started. "Do you understand why your mother is so upset?"

Sammy wiped his eyes with the back of his hand and nodded. "She's one of the hurt ones."

"The hurt... what?"

"She blames God for everything that's gone wrong in her life, so she's mad at Him. But she doesn't understand He's the one who loves her the most."

Mona chewed on her lip and tried to figure out a way to reason with Sammy. After all, now that she understood who had led him to this so-called faith, she needed to figure out a way to protect him. And her Raul. After a few moments, she sighed in frustration. "Sammy, why you can't be a good boy and forget about your God for a while? For your mother?"

Sammy shook his head. "No ma'am. It's because of my mom that I can't. I made a promise I have to keep."

Preacher could barely make out the road even though the windshield wipers raced across the glass on their highest speed. The rain tap-danced on the roof of the car, adding to their anxiety. He glanced at Raul in the passenger seat. "Are you okay?"

"I have a bad feeling, and it's not letting up."

"I feel it, too. Just keep praying we get there in time."

"We should go inside now," Mona said. "But you have to run so you don't get too wet."

Sammy nodded, shoved open the car door and stepped out into the storm. He stood there for a moment, not wanting to move. He didn't want to go inside to face his mom's disappointment in him, and it hurt him when she spoke so horribly about the God he had come to love so much. If he could only stay outside and avoid what he knew was coming, he would be willing to let the rain beat against him forever. But Mona stood impatiently on the porch waiting for him. Slowly, he made his way toward her.

"Samuél, walk faster! You will get sick like that."

He allowed her to usher him into the house and fuss over him with a towel. "Do you want some hot cocoa?"

He nodded and followed her to the kitchen. As soon as he entered the room, he knew. He turned and ran back through the house, calling her name even though he knew she wouldn't answer. "Mom!" His voice reverberated through the empty house, bouncing off the walls, and then falling back lifeless onto the floor. He ran back into the kitchen, where the storm pushed itself into the house through the open door.

It couldn't be. But it was. He was sure of it.

"Samuél," Mona said frantically. "Go take a hot bath while I look for your mother."

But Sammy was out the door before she'd even finished the sentence, running, racing, wildly pushing himself through the soggy sky toward the cliff.

Preacher threw the brakes on, and both he and Raul got out of the car and ran toward the house. When no one answered the door, they tried the knob and were relieved when the door pushed open. But as soon as they entered the house, they knew it was empty. Rushing wind and the sounds of the storm clamored through the house, and they followed them to the kitchen where they saw the back door swinging wildly in the wind.

"God help us," Raul said breathlessly. "I know where they are."

Chapter 13

By the time Gabriella reached the cliff, her peasant skirt and blouse were soaked through, and her hair clung to her face. She had lost both of her shoes, she now realized, during her frantic run from the house to the cliff. Instinct had driven her here, to this place of unreachable mysteries. To this cliff that held the power of life and death.

Gabriella felt emotionally spent, but even so, she raised her fists defiantly in the air as she watched the waves relentlessly assault the rocks below. "You don't fight fair," she sobbed, not even bothering to raise her voice, convinced no one could hear her anyway. "Why?" she asked. "Why must you have my son, too?"

She inched closer to the edge and felt some loose pebbles give way. She watched as they cascaded carelessly down the rocks until they disappeared into the water. Feeling strangely envious of the pebbles, a longing rose up inside of her. She wanted to join them in the bottom of the sea where she could lie in the stillness and not have to fight anymore. *It would be easier to allow myself to fall. At least then the pain would stop. God, I just want it to stop.* Gabriella felt a tempting limpness spread through her legs, making her realize how easy it would be to simply slip over the edge.

But then she thought of Sammy. *What kind of mother am I to even consider doing that to him?* He would carry the pain of it with him for the rest of his life and he would never get over losing her like that. She'd been a bad enough mother since Nicolas's death, but putting that kind of burden on him would be unforgivable. Gabriella took a step back from the edge, but her tears clouded and blurred her vision, making it impossible for her to understand just how close to the edge she really was.

Suddenly, a memory seared her mind and she recoiled from it. She had been five and alone in her parent's house for two days, waiting for them to return after their mysterious departure. The young Gabriella had been hungry, having already eaten the small amount of cooked food in the house. She was confused and scared, and she wandered the house going from room to room, window to window looking for the people who made up the whole of her life. She'd slept in her parent's bed since they'd been gone, determined not to miss them when they returned. Surely they would come back for her. Surely they would.

But they hadn't.

On the cliff, Gabriella felt the familiar ache well up inside of her. It was so recognizable, had been such a part of her for so long, and she realized that if she disappeared from Sammy's life, he would struggle with it, too. *I won't leave Sammy with that kind of pain.*

For a moment, she enjoyed the calmness that comes from making such a decision, and then an image of a woman intruded on her peace. The memory surprised her because she hadn't thought of the woman in years. Herlinda was her name, she remembered.

She had found Gabriella alone in the house after her parent's disappearance. The woman took her away in the dead of night and then gave the young Gabriella to her aunt who was living in the states. But even as a small child, Gabriella had sensed her aunt didn't want her. Knew her life would never again be the same.

The old feelings of pain and despair overwhelmed her again, and as Gabriella fought for relief from them, she realized that despite her best intentions, it was hopeless. As much as she wanted to give Sammy the kind of life she'd missed out on as a child, she couldn't. She was too broken, too torn up by life to be the kind of mom he needed.

She closed her eyes and let the tears of acceptance fall from her eyes as freely as the rain collapsing down around her. *I'm sorry Sammy, but you deserve more than me.*

As Sammy tore through the field, he heard the roar of the sea grow louder as he neared the cliff. It sounded angry and out of control, much like he felt now. Why couldn't his mom see the Truth? Why didn't she realize fighting against God was useless? *Give me a chance to be Your hands and feet,* he prayed. *Tell me how to show your love to my mom. She's a hurt one, Lord. Please don't let her fall over that cliff.* Sammy thought about what it would be like to go to Heaven and have to explain to his dad why his mom wasn't there, too, and it made him run even faster.

Thunder boomed, and the sky lit up. Sammy cried out when he saw his mom teetering on the edge of the cliff. "Hang on mom!" he cried. "Please! There are things you need to know."

Gabriella saw something out of the corner of her eye and stumbled when she realized it was Sammy. *How did he find her?* She looked tearfully at her son, and then let her gaze drift out to the sea, torn between a future she'd just given up on and the only way out she knew.

"Mom," Sammy cried. "Come away from there. I'm afraid you'll fall."

She looked at him, longed to be the kind of mother he needed, and felt anger at herself for not being able to do it. *What's wrong with me? Why can't I be like other mothers and just do what's best for my son?* Anguish smothered her heart when she thought about how feckless she'd become, and she realized with despair that if she couldn't get past the unrelenting pain that consumed her everyday, Sammy would experience the same thing as he grew older. And it would all be because of her.

"Go home, Sammy," she yelled into the wind. "I'll be home in a bit." She hoped with everything in her that she would. That she would find the strength to battle through another day.

But he shook his head stubbornly and made his way toward her along the outer edges of the cliff. He stumbled once then steadied himself against the slippery rocks and continued.

Panicked, Gabriella backed away from the cliff and started running toward him. "Sammy, stop! Those rocks are too slippery."

"Samuél, not so close to the edge," Mona cried as she approached.

Sammy jerked up his head in surprise, lost his balance, and then struggled to regain it. He looked from Mona to his mom, his eyes begging them to understand. Then he lost his footing and went over the edge.

Raul and Preacher came over the rise just in time to see Sammy disappear over the edge of the cliff. "Keep praying," Preacher boomed as he pushed his heavy body against the rain and toward the cliff. Raul, chest aching and barely able to move from shock, struggled to keep up.

Preacher moved agilely toward the edge where Gabriella now stood, gasping for the breath her sobs prevented. "Sammy!" she cried. "What have I done?"

Preacher looked down and felt a glimmer of hope when he realized Sammy had landed on an edge that jutted out from the wall of the cliff. "Okay, Lord," he breathed. "What would You have me do now?" He felt a hand on his shoulder and turned to find a devastated Raul. "Is he alive?"

Preacher shook his head. "There's only one way to know." He nimbly began the decent down the side of the cliff, seemingly without fear. He looked up before he was out of site. "Pray Raul. For the boy and for his mother."

Raul nodded, still unable to speak, unwilling to let his thoughts take him to what might be. He collapsed to his knees, bowed his head, crying out fervently for the lives of those he loved.

Gabriella crushed into Mona, her sobs forceful enough to tear apart the souls of all who heard them, and stood there hating God.

When Preacher reached the ledge, he slid toward Sammy scooting as close to him as he could. He leaned over and put his ear to Sammy's mouth. Breath. It was faint, but it was there. He looked up toward the others, shielding his eyes from the pelting rain, and yelled, "He's alive, but barely. Someone run back to the house and get a car out here. And call a doctor." He pulled Sammy tight against his barrel chest to shelter him from the punishing rain, and began the slow, steady climb to the top. With only man, it would have been impossible.

It was terrifying to watch Preacher slowly make his way up the cliff with Sammy, and Gabriella was trembling with the effort. He was alive. Her Sammy was alive, and there was hope.

When Preacher finally reached the top, Raul helped him get Sammy over the ledge and onto the ground. Preacher's face, red with the effort, was contorted with fear. "Cover him with something to protect him from the storm," he yelled.

Raul took off his raincoat, bent down beside Sammy, and laid it over him. He'd never seen Sammy so pale, and the boy's face was bleeding profusely. Gabriella sat bent over his head, and Raul heard her whispering "I'm sorry," over and over again. Mona had insisted on going for the car.

Preacher stood over them, his shirt soaked with Sammy's blood. "We must pray for the boy not to die. Now."

"Pray?" Gabriella's head shot up. "Leave your God out of this!"

"He's your son's God, too. And he needs His intervention desperately."

"You God has always taken from us, never given," she cried. "This time I won't let Him. He can't have my son."

Thunder cracked, and the lightning illuminated the sea. It looked restless, hungry, ready to swallow whatever was in its path.

"Maybe you don't understand," he said, his voice booming. "Without God's intervention, your son won't live. He's as good as dead now."

Gabriella grasped Sammy's hand and felt the warmth quickly fading.

She called to him and panicked when he didn't respond. Preacher came closer and leaned into her. "You're fighting Almighty God for your son, Gabriella. Don't you see that you're doing battle with the One who created him?"

Gabriella looked up, her swollen eyes pleading with him. "But if I give in, He'll take him from me. Don't you understand? Sammy is all I have left."

"That's fear driving you, Gabriella. God loves Sammy more than you ever could. He only wants what's best for him."

"No," she shook her head. "I don't believe you. I won't give God the chance to take him from me."

Preacher lowered his voice and knelt down beside her. "Understand me, Gabriella. You will never truly have Sammy until you release him to God."

She abruptly pulled away. "What are you saying? That it's wrong to be a mother to my child? To try and do what's best for him?"

He shook his head, frustrated because they were running out of time. "Exactly the opposite. I'm saying if you truly love him, you will put him in God's loving and able hands. Now."

She let out a sob and her face twisted in confusion. "I'm scared," she begged. "What if He takes him away from me?"

Preacher drew a deep breath. He knew he couldn't reassure her of something God never promised, but she needed to make a decision. Now. "If that's what happens it's because He knows something we don't. That's what faith is—letting Him make the call." He looked at Sammy's motionless, bleeding body. "What choice do you have, Gabriella?"

The truth of what he said slammed into her. She looked from him to Raul, who was nodding his head in solemn agreement, to Sammy's still body. Her little boy, who she loved so much, but was so utterly helpless to save. She took a deep breath and stood to face the sea. The unruly waves brutally hammered away at the rocks, giving them no relief. The rain, fragrant with fear, crushed down around her. The thunder collided with the sky. She closed her eyes and gave a half-nod, barely discernable to the others.

Gabriella only half understood what she was about to do. After all, she wasn't a believer. She couldn't have understood that the Host of Heaven stood by, silently urging her to utter the prayer that would put into motion the plan that was set before the beginning of time. There was no way for her to fathom what it meant to trust her child's life to God and His plan. She couldn't anticipate the gnawing pain of uncertainty, the painful releasing of her own will, the unimaginable loosening of her embrace. The awful, relentless letting go.

No, the only thing on Gabriella's mind at that moment was the life of her only son. The punishing rain whipped hard against her skin, and she felt the urging of unseen forces. A determined gust of wind compelled her to her knees—the tears of soul-understanding violently coursed down her cheeks.

"God, if you're really there" she whispered. "Please don't take my son away from me."

Gabriella paused, tried to quell the panic threatening to overwhelm her. The wind continued to push her to the ground. She swallowed roughly and lifted her eyes toward the sky. She was desperate, would do anything if only Sammy could live. Even petition this God she had grown to hate. "If you'll spare my Sammy, I promise to relinquish control of his future and put it into your hands. I make this oath to you: Let him live, and I'll give him back to you."

And so it was.

PART TWO:

One Week Later

Chapter 14

She wanted to believe. More than anything Gabriella wanted to believe God cared about her and Sammy, and that He desired good for them. She wished she could believe that she, Sammy and Nicolas would all be together again one day in Heaven. Even the possibility of it made her insides ache in a way she'd never experienced. To know that kind of love and the security that comes from it was something she'd longed for since she was five years old. But she'd lost it before and didn't trust it now. The risk of granting someone the ability to hurt her again, especially an all-powerful God, seemed unbearably impossible. Ridiculous, even.

Gabriella struggled with conflicting emotions. What if she gave in and believed in this God, and the entire thing turned out to be a lie? What if she naively put her trust in Him, and He in turn continued to destroy her? What if He expected too much of her? Asked her to do things she was incapable of? He might turn out to be a selfish God and expect her to give everything while He stood off afar and dispassionately watched her writhe in pain. What if He wasn't even real?

What would happen if He didn't act like she expected him to? Could she still love Him, or would His refusal to do things her way expose the thin veneer of her supposed faith? Could she really love this God? Or was she just so scared of Him she would profess to love him so He wouldn't completely destroy her?

And would He know the difference? Would He care?

What if she did trust Him, and He took her child away from her anyway?

Gabriella sighed in frustration. *I don't understand how faith is supposed to work.* After all, she wasn't talking about some esoteric exercise where the answer would never really affect her life. According to Sammy, her responses to these questions would determine the fate of her eternal life.

But she was torn. She was painfully aware of what she *should* believe, but for the most part, she was only pretending. After what happened on the cliff, everyone there assumed she had come to the faith. She had let them believe it, but if she were being completely honest with herself, she really didn't.

And as hard as she tried to make herself take on this truth as her own, she couldn't seem to do it. It seemed as if imperceptible forces had formed a barrier between her and this faith, this belief, and no matter how much she reached for it, her fingers always fell too short to grab hold of it.

But she'd seen the miracle for herself. She'd watched, stunned as Sammy opened his eyes and smiled after her prayer. "Mom," he said. "Your prayer sent me back."

Everyone had cheered, dropped to their knees and praised God for the miracle of Sammy's life. Everyone but Gabriella, who had stood there trembling uncontrollably. *Who is this God with so much power?* She wondered. *And what have I just done?*

But when Sammy's questioning eyes searched her out, she'd pushed aside her fear and panic, and she'd joined in the celebration. But since then, she'd kept one eye on those erratic heavens. *What would He do next?*

She'd felt emotionally unsteady for the week. Gabriella had been on edge, always expecting the great cosmic fist to thunder down from the sky and wreck something else. Expose the fake that she was. Punish her for holding out on Him in her heart. Surely this respite was temporary. It always was.

So she decided to keep pretending, to act as if she had given herself to this God who had given her back her son. She hoped that in time, maybe she'd truly grow to like Him. Trust Him just a little.

But Mona wasn't fooled. She had been retrieving the car when the miracle occurred and had to hear about it from the others. She was skeptical to say the least.

"Where is Samuél?" she asked now, brusquely slapping her paintbrush against the porch railing. She'd been unusually agitated lately.

"I expect him and Preacher any minute now. Remember? They went to San Abigail to preach today."

Mona shook her head. She desperately wanted to tell Gabriella about Preacher and his letter, but she promised Raul she would wait until he talked to the man. Raul thought Preacher was truly a man of God and would have an explanation for the letter, but Mona wondered. In the end, she had decided to respect Raul's wishes because Preacher had saved Samuèl. And if he meant to do him harm, he wouldn't have risked his own life to do that. "Foolishness," she uttered.

"I gave my word," Gabriella said. "Would you have me go back on it?"

"Absolutely," she snapped.

"You weren't there," Gabriella said, setting her paintbrush on the edge of the can. "It was a miracle. It's the only possible explanation for what happened. And that miracle was tied to the promise in my prayer."

"You have lost your mind, too."

"But I have my son."

Mona sighed. "I'm afraid for you, Gabriella. Afraid of what will happen when you realize the people of God are not who they pretend to be."

Gabriella closed her eyes, let the familiar fear wash over her. "Except now the people of God include my son. And Raul. And they sincerely believe God is real."

"Yes. They have been fooled as well."

She studied Mona's face and saw anger there, but she didn't think it was directed at God, but rather at the people who claimed to believe in Him. "You never told me what made you distrust Christians so much."

Mona set her paintbrush on the edge of the paint can and turned to face Gabby. "I know with certainty that some people who profess the faith are deceitful, and they may have done some very bad things in the past. I have held onto this knowledge for many years, but recently, it has taken on a greater importance for me."

"Why?"

She lowered her eyes. "Because I have always thought of it as being in the past. But now the past has caught up with the future, and I'm afraid people I love could get hurt."

"Mona, what is it?"

She sighed and shook her head in frustration. "I have to wait to tell you what I suspect."

"Mona, if there is something I need to know, you have to tell me."

She nodded slightly. "I know. But I promised Raul I wouldn't say anything about it yet. I think it's only right that I first talk to Raul about it again," she said. "I will speak to you when I'm sure. Bueno?"

"Raul knows what you suspect?"

"Yes, but he thinks I am wrong."

Gabriella took a deep breath and nodded. She wanted to hear what Mona had to say but fully understood her wanting to speak to Raul about her secrets before talking to anyone else. Gabriella decided not to let Mona's concerns overwhelm her as things always had in the past. Mona was suspicious of anyone who claimed a belief in God, and she suspected this would turn out be just another unfounded fear. Gabriella hoped Mona was wrong because she wanted to believe what Sammy did, and if she found out it was all a lie, she would truly be sorry.

She decided to let it go for now and give Mona the chance to speak to Raul. "Speaking of Raul," she said. "How is he feeling? Any better?" He hadn't been to the grove since Sammy's fall because he wasn't feeling well.

Mona shook her head. "Not so good. The doctor said his heart is tired."

Gabriella looked up sharply. "Mona, why didn't you tell me?"

She shrugged.

"But the doctor said he'll be okay, right? That all he needs is a little rest?"

Again, she shrugged.

"Oh Mona," Gabriella rushed to her and wrapped her arms tightly around her. "I'm sure he'll be fine. Raul is the strongest man I've ever known."

Mona nodded and wiped away a tear. "Do you think we can harvest the rest of the grove without him? The doctor says he shouldn't work until he's better."

"Of course we can. The men have done okay working the past few days without him. Will you ask Raul who I should put in charge?"

She nodded. "Bueno."

"And Mona? Do you think…I mean… shouldn't we pray for him or something?"

"No, I don't think so," she said sadly. She stood up and started down the stairs. "I will go now and check on Raul. We will finish the porch mañana, yes?"

As Gabriella watched Mona get into the car and pull away, she couldn't help sense things were only going to get worse before they got better.

Raul reached under the bed for the box. He needed to read the letter one more time before he decided what to do.

He took Preacher's old letter out of the box and prepared himself to read it again. It stunned him every time he read the words. In the restaurant the night of Sammy's fall, he'd asked Preacher about it, but they'd been interrupted by Gabriella before the man could answer, and he hadn't seen him since. But Preacher had recognized the letter. And now Raul felt driven to uncover its meaning. He put on his reading glasses and read the unsettling words again.

Señor Juarez,

I know you are a man of passion, and I admire you for it. I understand your reasoning about the tankers not being good for our environment, and now you are worried about the moral implications as well. But I believe there may be more to this issue than you're aware of. When we spoke about the things of God the other night, I came to know you as a reasonable man. You are also now my brother in Christ. I wonder if it might be possible to meet secretly so I can talk to you about something you should know. If you're willing, please come to the dock tonight at 11pm. Bring your wife as well.

I despise doing this secretively, but I'm afraid it's best for all those involved.

May God be with you,

Preacher

Raul sighed and let the piece of paper fall to his lap. No matter how many times he read it, the letter never failed to take his breath away. Preacher had been the one to lure Gabriella's parents away from the house that night. But why? It didn't make sense that he meant to do them harm. He was clearly a man of God and dedicated to doing His will. Soon after he left the letter for the Juarezes, Preacher had spent his entire life traveling from town to town telling people about God's love. Why would a man like that think to harm innocent people? He had also risked his very life to save Samuél. But still. The letter raised a lot of questions in Raul's mind.

Raul gently placed the letter back inside the box. *What was what Preacher's role in all of this?* No matter how much his heart told him Preacher was a good man, and no matter how much he wanted to trust him, Raul held evidence in his hands that he'd been the one to pull Gabriella's parents away from their home the night they disappeared. And Mona. How did she come to have the letter?

"Where did you find that?"

Raul looked up to find Mona with a look of disgust on her face. "I guess I found it where you left it."

"So you see," she said, moving toward him. "Your man of God isn't what he appears to be after all."

Raul nodded. "It seems he's got some questions to answer, I'll agree with that."

"Some questions?" she said, struggling to keep her voice from rising. "Esposo, he's pretending to be someone he's not. Ingratiating himself into a family he likely destroyed many years ago. Don't you wonder why he's attached himself to the grandson of the people he most likely hurt?"

Raul looked up sharply. "Samuél? You think he means to do him harm?"

She regretted saying it the instant the words came out of her mouth. The color rose quickly in Raul's face and a tiny white line appeared around his lips as he pressed them together. "No, esposo," she said, walking over and taking the box from him. "I'm sure he means Samuél no harm. But I would like to hear his explanation about why he left the letter for the Juarezes."

Raul got out of bed, and when Mona tried to stop him he gently pushed her away.

"Raul! Where are you going?"

At first, she thought he was falling, but before Mona could move to catch him, he knelt down on his knees and extended his hand out toward hers. "We must pray for Samuél's protection," he said, slightly out of breath.

Mona stood still, unsure of what to do.

"Esposa," he said sharply. "Give me your hand."

She held out her hand and allowed him to pull her down next to him. Unsure of herself, she tentatively knelt there and pitied Raul as he made desperate entreaties to who he believed was the Creator of Heaven and Earth. His eyes were closed as he prayed, so he never saw Mona who was refusing to pray and instead staring out the window watching the wind chase the clouds across the sky.

Preacher came to an abrupt stop, his old farm truck skidding as the bald tires battled against the gravel for traction.

"Lo siento! I'm sorry," said Juan Jose as he dodged the skidding truck.

"You could have been hit," Preacher said.

"I know, but I've been waiting for Samuél for hours because his mom said he'd be back today from San Abigail. But I couldn't wait to see him, so I've been sitting under this tree all day. And when I saw your truck I got so excited I jumped into the road without thinking."

Preacher took a deep breath, exhausted from trying to keep up with the boy's rapid fire speech.

"Climb in Juan Jose," said Sammy. "You can ride with us back to the house." He quickly glanced at Preacher, who nodded his approval.

Juan Jose bounded up the side rail and flopped onto the seat next to Sammy. "Samuél, where have you been? Ever since you fell off the cliff, I haven't been able to see you."

"I know, me and Preacher have been going to a lot of different towns to talk about God. Hey," he said, sitting up straighter. "Maybe you could come with us to the next one."

They both looked at Preacher.

"I don't see why not," he said. "You could help with the preparations. Of course, you'll have to get permission from your mother."

The boys high-fived each other. "When do we leave?" asked Juan Jose.

"First thing in the morning."

"Oh." He slumped in his seat.

"What's wrong?"

"My mamá told me I have to finish repairing the chicken coop tomorrow because Raul is sick and he can't do it, and—"

"—Raul's sick?" asked Sammy. "What's wrong with him?"

"I'm not sure."

Sammy looked at Preacher. "I want to go see Raul."

But Preacher had already slowed down the truck and began to do a U-turn in the middle of the road.

She hadn't been to the cliff since Sammy's fall, and Gabriella approached it with trepidation. The sea no longer felt dark and unpredictable, but rather mystifying, and she felt unsure of it. She wasn't sure if it would unexpectedly go from calm to tempest, from merciful to spiteful. Gabriella was surprised to find she had lost the urge to fall over the cliff. And she no longer wanted to push fate and stand so close to the edge, but instead stood back at a safe distance. *Was I ever really that close?*

For the first time, she saw the way the sun bounced along the water, making it shimmer. It looked almost... hopeful. She took a step back and let her eyes drift toward the horizon, that place where everything begins and ends, and let herself wonder what she'd find if she could go there. The breeze lifted the edges of her skirt, playful and flirtatious, and sent a welcomed chill down her spine in the heat of the day.

The wind picked up and began to blow menacingly, and along with it came the memories. It all mingled and swirled, wrapping itself tighter and tighter around her until she could hardly breathe. You've hoped before, the wind cruelly whispered. And look what happened. Your parents. Nicolas. His parents.

"But Sammy," she cried out to the spinning chaos around her. "He's alive against all hope."

Lies, the wind hissed. A set up for a fall.

"God, if you're there," she pleaded. "Please tell me what to do." A seagull swooped down, cawing loudly, and she watched as it rolled in the wind, the feathers on its wing fluttering like the pages of a book. She smiled and walked away from the cliff. She knew just what she had to do.

Raul heard the truck coming up the road and sat up in bed. His chest had been heavy all afternoon, and he didn't know if it was his heart or the sense of dread he couldn't seem to shake. He'd felt unsettled ever since he tried to pray with his wife. Her coldness toward God had never been clearer to him, and he thought he might finally understood why. If she believed Preacher was responsible for the death of Gabriella's parents and then the cover up, how could she believe anything he said about God? From her perspective, he and Sammy had been converted by a fraud. He closed his eyes and sank into himself. *Whatever it takes, Lord. Bring Mona to Your saving grace. Protect Sammy and show me the truth about Preacher.*

"Company," Mona said from the doorway. "I don't recognize the truck. Are you expecting anyone?"

He shook his head.

"Well then, I'll just run them off."

"Wait," he said, pushing back the covers. "Let's see who it is."

He heard car doors slamming and then energetic feet clomping up the stairs. "Raul! Raul! Are you here? It's Sammy!"

Raul smiled and headed toward the door, but stopped abruptly when he realized Preacher would be with Sammy because they'd probably just driven in from San Abigail. Mona stood in front of the door frozen, watching as Preacher made his way up the porch stairs. Raul nodded at her and pulled open the door. Sammy came in like a swift tide and threw himself into Raul.

"Raul! I heard you were sick. What's wrong? Are you okay?"

"I'm fine Samuél. The doctor wants me to rest my heart for a little while, and then I'll be back to the grove."

Sammy pulled away from Raul. "Your heart?" He put his head against Raul's chest, closed his eyes and listened. "I hear it," he whispered. "It sounds tired." Sammy looked up. "I'm scared, Raul."

"God did not give us a spirit of fear, son." Preacher stood in the doorway.

"Well, he sure did give us enough to be afraid of," Mona said, talking Sammy's arm and pulling him away from the man. "Let's go to the kitchen. I just pulled some cookies out of the oven. You too, Juan Jose."

Sammy looked to Raul, who nodded his approval, and reluctantly followed Mona and Juan Jose into the kitchen.

Raul turned toward Preacher, the man who had given him his cherished faith and life everlasting, and he felt nothing but warmth. Raul knew. Whatever happened, he was sure Preacher was a good man.

"You have questions," Preacher said.

"Yes, my brother. I need you to put my concerns to rest."

Preacher nodded and walked toward the living room where he eased his bulky frame into a chair facing the sofa. Raul followed and sank gratefully into the deep cushions on the sofa. The two men looked at each other for a long moment, and then Preacher let out a tired breath. "I guess I've got some explaining to do. About the letter, I mean."

Raul nodded slowly, expectantly.

"There are things about those days you don't know. In fact, only three living people do."

Raul sat up straighter. "Living?"

Preacher held up his large hand. "I'll get to that, Raul. I have to tell the story in my own way."

Raul nodded and leaned back against the soft cushions.

"You see, while the battle for the dock was certainly about whether or not the village would increase in prosperity and size, there was more to it. It was also about the lives of men. That's what I was trying to tell the Juarezes the night they disappeared.

"The fact is, I agreed with Ignacio Juarez. The dock would have certainly attracted an element to the area that would have brought rapid moral decay to our little village. Why, it was already happening. The Castinoles, the family who used to live up on the hill, purchased land near the dock and were planning to build a cantina. So while I didn't disagree with Mr. Juarez, I knew about something else happening in the village he wasn't aware of. Something darker. Times had gotten so tough around here men weren't able to support their families anymore. Some of them tried to get jobs in the neighboring towns, but not many of them succeeded. It was a difficult time for many families, and so of course, unscrupulous people began to appear. But the worst of them were the coyotes."

"The people who take men across the border for a fee?"

"Yes, and most of them did just that. They offered illegal passage into the U.S. where the men could work in the fields and send money home to their families."

"But Preacher, that's been happening for generations. Many men have gone to the United States in order to support their families during tough times."

"Yes, but this was different. You see, a large number of men who left were never heard from again."

"I remember that, but we all assumed it was part of the risk. Everyone knows it's a dangerous trip."

Preacher nodded. "That was the beauty of the plan. Everyone assumed that. What made it even more perfect is that the authorities would never investigate. Think about it. Who would the families of the men call—the Mexican or U. S. authorities? The victims were in the process of breaking the law, so who would fight for them?"

"Victims?"

Preacher nodded, leaned forward and lowered his voice. "The men who disappeared were never heard from again." He looked pointedly at Raul. "And they weren't the type of men to run off from their families."

Raul sucked in his breath and brought his hand to his chest. "What happened to them?"

Preacher shrugged. "That's what I was trying to find out the night the Juarezes disappeared." He saw the look of confusion on Raul's face. "Maybe I'd better back up. I started to notice a pattern with the men who were disappearing. As far as I've been able to put it together, every man who left and didn't come home had approached the bank for a loan to help get through the tough times. In every case, the loan was granted with the family property used as collateral. The men left for the states, perhaps to earn enough money to support their families and repay the loan, and when they didn't return, the bank foreclosed on the property as soon as the loan went into default. Typically, the bank would then lease the property back to the man's family. So you see, if the dock had indeed come to town, the bank would have owned much of the town's real estate. My guess is that they would have kicked out the families, sold the properties to the highest bidder, and made some money. But since the dock was never completed, the bank continues to lease the properties to the families and pockets the rents every month."

Raul whistled. "So, you think the people who own the bank caused the men's disappearances to steal their property? But I thought you and Hector Mendez were friends?"

"Friends? No. But I did try and get to know him in order to figure out what was happening to the men. I suspected his involvement, but I could never find anything to confirm it."

"So you don't have any proof of this?"

Preacher shook his head. "No, but..." He looked toward the kitchen and lowered his voice. "You know Juan Jose's father is one of the men who haven't been heard from. But do you also know his mother has rented from the bank ever since his disappearance?"

"Yes, but he disappeared only a few years ago."

Preacher nodded. "That's what I'm afraid of. It's continuing."

"But I don't understand. The possibility of the docks being built went away a long time ago."

Preacher nodded. "That means there's something more. Something I haven't figured out yet. Whatever reason Mendez has for wanting all the property in our little village still exists."

"But how can we possibly find out what it is?"

"Remember, there are a few people who know what's going on."

"Yes, but who are they?"

"Me of course, Hector Mendez, and Hector's wife, and well… I guess you make four."

Raul nodded. "Herlinda. I remember Hector's wife."

Preachers' eyes widened. "You knew her?"

"Not really. I only met her once. The night she came to take away Gabriella after her parent's disappearance. She told me she had located her aunt who had agreed to raise Gabriella. I never saw her again. I heard she died shortly after that."

"Yes, that's what they say."

"You don't believe it?"

"I'm not sure. I've been trying to track her down for years. If she is still alive, she could be the key that unlocks the mystery of the missing men."

Raul nodded slowly. "I still don't understand how all of this relates to the disappearance of Gabriella's parents."

"You see, the fire in their grove drastically reduced their income, and they had decided to go to the bank for a loan for the money to replant the grove. Mr. Juarez was planning to go to the U.S. to work for a short time until they could recover financially from the fire. They told me this the night we talked about God. They had an appointment at the bank the next day. I left them the note because I wanted to warn them."

"They were going to Mendez for money? They must have been desperate."

Preacher nodded. "Losing half of their grove was a big deal in such hard times. You worked for them—didn't they tell you the financial shape they were in?"

Raul shook his head. "No, they never missed a paycheck for either me or Mona. They acted like everything was fine."

Preacher drew in a deep breath. "Which leads me to my next question, brother." He looked towards the ground. "If the Juarezes had received my note that night, they may not have disappeared." He looked up at Raul and softened his voice. "I need to know how Mona ended up with it."

Mona quickly stacked the cookies onto a plate, careful not to let them burn her fingertips. She poured three glasses of milk and sat at the table with Sammy and Juan Jose. The brightly colored blouse that she wore contrasted sharply with the gray pinstriped skirt that had once been a part of a corporate suit. She kicked off her work boots and studied Sammy.

"Samuél, it will be okay. Raul is a strong man."

"I know," Sammy said softly. "But he looks so tired."

Mona nodded and turned toward the window. It had become increasingly clear to her that Raul wasn't getting better, no matter how much he rested. When she felt the tears threaten to come, she quickly pushed them back down. The last thing she wanted to do was worry the boys. She would have to work harder to make him better, she decided. She began to mentally make a list of the meals she would prepare for him in the next few days in order to help his heart heal more quickly.

"I talked to Maria," Juan Jose blurted out. "She says she needs to see you."

"Okay. Where?"

"I don't know. I figured you would."

"Maria?" Mona said. "Who is this girl, Samuél?"

Sammy's face turned a deep shade of red. He shrugged. "It's nothing."

"Nothing?" said Juan Jose. "It's nothing that you're speaking of the woman you're going to marry?"

"Oh? We're going to have a wedding, are we?" Mona, glad for the distraction, lifted herself out of the chair. "I guess I'd better pull out my wedding cake recipes." She winked at Juan Jose as she pulled down a well-used cookbook.

Sammy groaned, sank deeper into his chair and shot a threatening look at his friend.

"Can I be your best man?" Juan Jose asked, ignoring the warning look. "I've never worn a tuxedo before."

Sammy rolled his eyes.

"How is your mother?" Mona asked Juan Jose, finally putting an end to Sammy's misery.

"She is very frustrated about the chicken coop. The nesting boxes are broken, so the hens keep laying their eggs where we can't find them. We've had to eat avena seven mornings in a row." He scrunched up his nose.

Mona nodded. "I'd do it myself, but I'm afraid to leave Raul for that long. I'll try and find someone else to do it."

"We could do it with Preacher's help, and I bet we could finish it before we leave town tomorrow," Sammy said.

"Yes, and then we can ask my mamá about me going with you."

"I'll ask him," Sammy said, jumping up and heading for the door.

"Wait," Mona said. "Let the men finish talking. Then you can ask your Preacher."

"Tienas Biblias?" Gabriella asked the bookstore owner.

"Bibles? Yes, we have a great assortment over here." The tall woman led her to some shelves stacked with Bibles. "Which translation are you looking for?"

"Translation?"

"You know, Revision Reina-Valera or one written in more modern language?"

"Aren't they all the same?"

The woman considered Gabriella for a moment. "I think I have just the right Bible for you." She reached for one, pulled it out and showed Gabriella the study notes. She told her how they would help explain the passages she didn't understand.

"Perfect." Gabriella followed the woman to the counter and paid for the Bible.

Once in the car, she held the book tenderly and closed her eyes. "God," she whispered. "You spoke to me once before from this book, even though I didn't realize it at the time." She thought back to the verse that had shown her where Sammy was when he snuck out to the revival. "I need you to do it again. Please?" She set the book on her lap and let it fall open. Then she placed her finger on the page and opened her eyes.

"'Have I not commanded you? Be strong and courageous. Do not be frightened, and do not be dismayed, for the LORD your God is with you wherever you go.'"

Thrilled, Gabriella threw back her head, tears of joy streaming down her face. "Okay, okay," she said. "You're beginning to grow on me."

Raul looked fully into Preacher's eyes. "I can't answer that question, but I can say this with absolute certainty: however Mona came to have that note, it will not reflect poorly on her. She may not be a believer… yet, but she's a good, honest woman through and though."

Preacher considered it for a moment and nodded. "That's good enough for me."

Raul visibly relaxed. "I'll ask her how she came to have it. That's where we'll get some answers."

"That sounds like a reasonable plan," he said hefting his body out of the chair. "We've got a lot to do before we leave in the morning, so we better get to it."

Raul put his hand on Preacher's knee. "Wait, there's something more."

"Oh?" he said, sitting back down.

"I'm afraid for Mona, for her salvation. I want to pray with you in agreement for her."

"Of course, Raul. But you realize I pray for her everyday."

Raul shook his head. "Not like this. This is something the Holy Spirit is leading me to do."

Preacher nodded solemnly, clasped Raul's hands and bowed his head.

"Lord," Raul began. "Creator of Heaven and Earth, You who give life and take it away, You, who in your mighty love, desire that no one should die without knowing you as their Savior, I come to You on behalf of my precious esposa. Lord, you know she's a good woman, but..." His voice cracked. He took a deep breath and continued. "That's not enough for her to enter your kingdom on the day she passes from this earth. My soul aches with the knowledge that she doesn't know You for who You are.

"Lord, I willingly submit myself to whatever it takes to bring her into Your kingdom."

Preacher jerked up and withdrew his hands. His eyes were wide with revelation. "Raul. Do you understand what you're doing? The Holy Spirit has just given me understanding..."

"I know exactly what I'm doing," he said evenly.

"Well, I'll be," he said softly. He drew in a deep breath and once again extended his hands to Raul, only now he was trembling with the knowledge of what was to come.

"Whatever it takes," Raul prayed forcefully. "Whatever it takes."

Chapter 15

Preacher, Sammy and Juan Jose all climbed into the battered old truck and took off down the dirt road. The boys watched as Raul and Mona stood in the doorway, waving until they appeared smaller and smaller. Finally, the couple disappeared from sight.

Sammy turned to Juan Jose. "Do you think your mom will let you go with us tomorrow?"

"She might say yes if we fix the coop before we leave." He looked at Preacher. "Do you think we can finish it today?"

But Preacher continued to stare straight ahead, thoughtfully tapping his thumb against the steering wheel.

"Preacher?"

"Hmm? Did you say something?"

"Do you think it's possible to finish repairing the coop today?"

"Well, it depends on how much work is involved." He turned the truck onto a narrow dirt path. "We're here, so let me take a look at it and I'll let you know, okay?"

As soon as the truck came to a stop, Sammy and Juan Jose jumped out. "Come on, we'll show you where it is."

He lumbered after them and stopped short when he saw the coop. It was obvious Raul had started the work, but he had been rebuilding the entire coop rather than only replacing the broken nesting boxes. There was still a lot to do.

"What do you think?" They asked in unison.

Preacher blew out his breath hard. "It looks like a lot of work, boys. We'd better get started if we have any chance of finishing by dark."

"Yes!" they yelled before high-fiving each other.

The screen door on the main house slapped open, and Rosa called out in Spanish, "Juan Jose, come here!"

"I'm coming, mamá!" he said as he ran toward her.

Preacher and Sammy pulled out the tools and new wood Raul had stored for the project. "Let's continue with Raul's plan," Preacher said. "See how he was tearing out these boards and replacing them with the new wood in sections? I think that's the best approach."

They worked together by popping out the old, rusted nails and taking down the rotted boards. They were putting up the first new board when Juan Jose came running back.

"Samuél! My mamá said yes!"

"She did?"

"But only if we finish the coop."

"Look, we've already started!" Sammy held the new board in place so Preacher could nail it in to place.

"There," the older man said. "Only about a hundred to go." He looked at his watch. "We'd better get busy."

They worked for hours, barely stopping for a break, even when Juan Jose's mamá brought out freshly squeezed orange juice and fish tacos. But no matter how optimistic they tried to be, they couldn't hide their disappointment when the sun's light faded before they'd completed the job.

"Bueno," said Juan Jose sadly when he could no longer see the nails in the old boards. "We tried our best. I guess I'll finish it by myself in the morning."

"Giving up that easily?" Preacher boomed.

"But we can't even see the nails anymore. How can we keep working?"

"Wait here."

The boys watched as Preacher ambled off toward his truck and then pulled it directly in front of the coop. He got out, leaving the headlights on. "How's that?"

"Perfect!"

The boys quickly found the nails and began pulling them out, and it wasn't long before they found their rhythm again. A few hours later, Juan Jose hammered in the last nail. "There, you silly hens," he yelled. Now you are forever condemned to laying your eggs where we can find them!"

"We'd better go up to the house and let your mother know we finished. I'm sure she'll have questions about the trip."

They wearily climbed into the truck, and just as Preacher was about put it in reverse, he stopped. "Wait, what's that? Did we leave some nails on the ground?"

"No sir," said Sammy. "We picked them all up and put them in the box."

"Then what's that glint? Over there where we stacked all the old wood?" Preacher put the gear into neutral and climbed out. A few moments later, he came back holding a small tin box. "Juan Jose, do you recognize this? It was partially buried over there where we were working."

"Yes sir," he said solemnly. "That box belongs to my papá."

"Well, I'll be." Preacher stared at the box, obviously perplexed. "I wonder why he would have buried it out here?"

"Should we look inside?" Sammy asked.

"Yes, Samuèl! Maybe it contains the clue we've been looking for that will tell us where he is. And then we can decide which of our plans we'll use to bring him home."

Preacher slowly shook his head. "No, I don't think it's our place. Why don't we take it inside and let Juan Jose's mother decide what to do with it."

"Can I carry it to her?" Juan Jose asked softly.

Preacher handed the small metal box to him. "It's yours to carry, son."

The three didn't speak during the short trip up the gravel drive to the house, but Preacher noticed Juan Jose stealthily wiping at his eyes while pretending to stare out the window. He held the box protectively against his body.

Lord, he prayed silently. *What have I uncovered? Whatever it is, please let it bring this boy some peace about his father.*

The screen door slapped open as soon as they reached the house and Rosa walked out onto the porch. "You are finished?"

"Yes mamá, we're finished. But look, we found papá's box buried next to the coop."

"What? Let me see it."

They all went inside the house and gathered in the small, meticulously scrubbed living room. The furniture was mismatched and threadbare, but it was arranged to create a cozy atmosphere. A large photograph of Juan Jose and his parents dominated the tiny room, and crosses hung above every doorway. They sat around the low wooden table, all looking expectantly at Juan Jose, who seemed reluctant to let go of the box.

"Give it to me," his mother said quietly.

He hesitantly placed it in the middle of the table. Rosa picked it up and tried to pull off the tin lid, but it was so tight she had to shake the box to get it off. Once it was open, she sat still and stared at the contents. A single piece of paper in a perfect square sat in the middle of the box.

"Would you like some privacy, Senora?"

"No se. I don't know."

With visibly shaking hands, she took the paper out of the box and spread it open on her lap. Her eyes scanned it quickly, and then looked up, a look of confusion on her face.

Preacher, seeing her emotion, started to rise. "Let's give her some privacy."

She shook her head. "No, it's not necessary." She held out the paper to Preacher. "I don't understand what this is."

Preacher took the piece of paper and read it. "Senora, do you know this woman? Herlinda Mendez?"

"Yes," she answered. "She is the wife of the banker, Hector Mendez. But why would my husband bury her name and address in our yard?"

"I don't know. When is the last time you saw her?"

"The night my husband left for the United States. She met with him here."

"What did she want?"

"I'm not sure. It seemed urgent, but my husband told me not to worry. He said she was upset about something, but it didn't have anything to do with us."

"I don't recognize the name of this town. Do you?"

"El Perdido? Yes. It's about five hours south of here, right off the main highway."

Preacher leaned back against the sofa. "Senora, I'd like to change our plans. If it's all right with you, we'll head to El Perdido first thing in the morning for our next revival."

She looked at Juan Jose. "Is this okay with you?"

"Yes mamá. It might give us some answers about papá."

When Preacher pulled up to Sammy's house, Gabriella was waiting on the porch, worried because she'd expected them home much earlier.

As soon as Preacher realized he'd forgotten to call Gabriella to tell her they'd be late, he jumped out of the truck. "I'm sorry," he said as he made his way to the porch. "We lost track of time. Will you forgive me for not calling to let you know we'd be late?"

"I was worried," Gabriella said, motioning Sammy over. "Promise me it won't happen again?"

When Preacher assured her it wouldn't, she visibly relaxed.

It had been a long, tiring day and Sammy let himself be pulled into her embrace, too tired to be embarrassed about it. Preacher apologized some more and filled her in on their plans before leaving to get a good night's sleep in preparation for their trip.

"Sleepy?" she asked as she guided Sammy inside.

"Exhausted."

"I told Preacher I would call him when you woke up in the morning. I think you need a good night's sleep after such a long day."

"Thanks, mom."

"That will give us some time for a little something else I've planned after breakfast."

Sammy perked up. "What is it?"

She smiled. "It's a surprise. Now why don't you take a shower and climb into bed?"

After Sammy was clean and sleeping soundly, Gabriella sat at the desk in front of The Book. "Okay, God," she muttered under her breath. "This was Your idea. Teach me what I need to know."

Chapter 16

"Mmmm, that smells good. I'm starving."

Gabriella smiled. "Good morning sleepy head. I thought you were going to sleep all the way until lunch."

"Did you talk to Preacher?"

She nodded. "A little while ago. He said you guys would wait to leave until early this afternoon. He's going to use the time to pick up some supplies in town." She set down a large plate of pancakes and eggs in front of Sammy. He leaned over it, inhaled deeply, and picked up his fork to cut into the stack.

"Aren't you going to thank God for that food?"

Sammy's fork stopped mid-air. "Huh?"

Gabriella shrugged. "It seems rude not to, don't you think? The Bible says everything we have comes from Him."

"Um, mom? Are you okay?"

Gabriella laughed and turned toward the sink. "I'm fine Sammy." And she was. In fact, she felt better than she had in years.

Sammy bowed his head, said a quick prayer of thanks and quickly ate everything on his plate. "Okay," he said after he'd taken the last bite. "What's the surprise?"

Gabriella cleared away the dishes and picked up a book and a stack of notes. She sat down next to Sammy. "You asked me a question when your dad died, and at the time, I didn't have an answer for you." She opened the book to the page she'd marked and looked at him. "But now I think I do."

"Um… is that a Bible?"

Gabriella nodded.

"And you've been reading it?"

"Yes."

"Wow."

"Don't look so surprised," she said, laughing. "I'm investigating things for myself, and frankly, I like what I'm finding."

Sammy pumped his fist in the air. "Yes!" Then he turned serious. "What was the question, mom? Was it about dad?"

Gabriella nodded, ran her finger along the page and held it there to mark it. "After your dad died, you asked me if we would ever see him again, and I didn't know how to answer you. But I found this last night in the Bible. 'But we do not want you to be uninformed brothers, about those who are asleep.'" Gabriella looked up. "My study Bible says the word "asleep" mean the same as died for those people who believed in Jesus." She found her place again and continued reading.

"'But we do not want you to be uninformed, brothers, about those who are asleep, that you may not grieve as others do who have no hope. For since we believe that Jesus died and rose again, even so, through Jesus, God will bring with him those who have fallen asleep. For this we declare to you by a word from the Lord, that we who are alive, who are left until the coming of the Lord, will not precede those who have fallen asleep. For the Lord himself will descend from heaven with a cry of command, with the voice of an archangel, and with the sound of the trumpet of God. And the dead in Christ will rise first. Then we who are alive, who are left, will be caught up together with them in the clouds to meet the Lord in the air, and so we will always be with the Lord. Therefore encourage one another with these words.' Gabriella looked up. "Do you understand what this means?"

Sammy nodded. "It means if we believe what Jesus says, we'll see dad again in Heaven when we die."

Gabriella wiped away a runaway tear. "It almost sounds too good to be true, doesn't it?"

"But it is."

"How can you be so sure, Sammy?"

He shrugged. "Because I can feel Him love me."

"Who? Your dad?"

"Uh-uh. God."

Gabriella sighed. "I wish it could be as real for me as it is for you. I wonder if it will ever happen?"

Sammy smiled. "Mom, I'm pretty sure it's already beginning."

A few hours later, Gabriella watched a cloud of dust rise on the sandy drive as Preacher, Sammy and Juan Jose sped off to yet another town to preach the Word of God. She took a sip of her tea and swallowed it around the lump in her throat. She realized she was supposed to trust God to do what was best for Sammy, and she'd promised Him she would allow Sammy to live his life according to His will, but the voice of doubt was relentless. She fought the urge to chase after the truck and pull Sammy safely back into the house. She walked to the porch swing, sat down and comforted herself with the knowledge that school would start soon, and she'd have Sammy home where he belonged.

Unless of course, God had other plans.

"God," she whispered. "This is too hard. How can you expect a woman to put aside all of her motherly instincts and trust you?" Instantly, she remembered Mary, the mother of Jesus. How her heart must have broken as she watched her child endure all He had while she had been helpless to do anything about it. Gabriella put her head in her hands and offered the cry of her heart. "So you do expect this of me. Show me how I can possibly do this willingly."

Gabriella's spotted another cloud of dirt, this one coming toward her. It was Mona. Things had been a little strained between them since she had offered to pray for Raul, but Gabriella was determined to make things right between them. The car came to an abrupt halt in front of the yellow house and a mass of stripes, plaids and flowers, all in mismatched colors, got out. Gabriella, who was about to say the first words to mend their strained friendship, froze when she saw the utter wildness in Mona's eyes.

"I need help," the older woman said, the wind carrying her words to Gabriella's ears like a slap. "It's my Raul. I think he is dead."

Raul felt the weight of every regret, every burden and worry lift instantaneously from his shoulders. He was pulled, surrounded and serenaded by a love he could have never imagined on earth. And even though he was in the midst of it, he still found it difficult to comprehend. Swirls of mercy and grace and forgiveness and long-suffering circled around him and made him want to stay in this place forever. But there was a pull, a promise of something better, if that were possible, awaiting him. He followed the love, moved toward the irresistible presence that beckoned him. And when he came into that presence, he immediately fell on his face, overcome by the majesty of his King.

"My Lord and my God."

The King gently touched him, and Raul found himself standing before the One he had faithfully served in his last days on earth.

"Lord, I'm so ashamed. I wasted so many years living in rebellion to You."

"So the last will be first, and the first last."

"But Lord, what about my Mona?"

The King smiled at him, and His eyes set off a trillion rays of light. "Is My arm too short to save?"

Instantly, Raul realized the foolishness of his question. "No, Lord."

"There is no greater love than a man who would lay down his life for his friends."

Raul knelt down before Him and bowed his head. "I am forever grateful for your sacrifice, Lord."

"I was speaking of yours."

Raul looked up in surprise. "Mine?"

"Your heartfelt prayer was heard."

Raul nodded, realizing that He was talking about the prayer he and Preacher had prayed for Mona's salvation. *Whatever it takes.* "I heard the prompting in my spirit to offer that prayer."

"You heard well, my good and faithful servant. Now come, enter into the joy of your Lord."

Raul fell into the embrace of his King, and he was filled with the knowledge that he'd entered a realm of utter joy and mystery and love and adventure that no human being has ever imagined.

And it would never end.

"Oh no," said Gabriella, rushing down the stairs and hugging a trembling Mona. "Tell me what happened."

"No time," she said frantically. "You must come now."

Gabriella didn't bother locking the door or even grabbing her purse. Instead, she hurried with Mona toward the car. "Let me drive," she said, gently taking the keys.

Mona nodded and walked numbly to the passenger side where she collapsed inside of the car.

They didn't speak on the way to the house. Gabriella because she was too concerned about what was happening. Surely Raul wasn't dead. He had probably passed out, but even so, they needed to get to him and take him to the doctor.

And Mona didn't speak because she couldn't find a way to form the words. Instead, she stared out the window at the passing cliffs and patches of sea. The beach roses were in full bloom, their pretty pink petals belied the reality of what was happening. *How is it possible for both life and death to exist on this dreadful day?* But the thought left her as carelessly as it had come, slipping out the window and mingling with the sorrowful sea air.

Gabriella pulled in front of the house and turned off the engine. She looked at the house Raul and Mona had lived in for their entire marriage. It sagged a little, like its occupants, but was strong at its core where it matters. She swung open the car door and had started up the path leading to the porch stairs before she realized Mona hadn't moved. Gabriella decided to go in alone to see for herself what was going on. She opened the front door and cautiously went inside.

She sensed it immediately. It wasn't a presence she felt, but rather the absence of one. Raul was gone, she was certain of it. Anxiously, she made her way toward the back of the house to the bedroom. The door was open, and an open window had allowed the humid breeze from the sea to permeate the room. Raul was stretched out on the bed, looking as if he were asleep, except for his absolute stillness. Gabriella moved toward him, unable to look away from the almost rapturous look on his face.

"Oh, Raul." She sat next to him and placed her hand on his face, felt the cold, the stillness of his skin. "Why did you have to leave us now?" Raul's shirt was damp, and she rose to close the window, thinking the sticky, wet air was the cause, but realized the dampness had come from her tears. She wiped her eyes, but the tears didn't stop. They kept coming and coming. And coming.

Gabriella looked at Raul's aged face and thought of the younger, stronger Raul of her youth. She hadn't known him well then—she was just a child—but she remembered his steadfast presence in the grove, and how her father had relied on him to nurture the orange trees. When she thought of Raul's kindness in caring for the grove after her parents died and she was taken away, she cried even harder. It was an act of honest loyalty and friendship from a man who had lived his life for others. She was glad they'd had the opportunity to become close since her return, but she wished there had been more time.

Gabriella picked up the phone from the bedside table and made arrangements for someone to come and get Raul. Then she sat in the corner chair and tried to pull herself together. She wasn't ready to face Mona, who was sitting silently in the car. How could the poor woman do anything else? She could barely cope herself.

Tell her about the verse.

"What?" Gabriella looked around the room, but didn't see anyone. She got up and walked to the living room, wondering if the coroners had arrived, but the house was empty. *I must be hearing things*, she thought.

Tell her. About the verse.

She looked around. "What verse?"

Suddenly a flood of memories from that morning came rushing at her. She and Sammy had talked about this very thing. That those who fell asleep believing in Christ will live again.

Wait a minute, she thought. *Am I hearing from God?* A second later, a hysterical laughter rose up inside of her. "Yeah right," she said under her breath. "I'm having a conversation with God."

Her thoughts turned to Mona sitting alone in the car, and she made her way to the door. She needed to get to Mona before the coroners arrived and be strong for her friend.

Juan Jose, bring your arm back inside the truck, Preacher said. "I want to return you to your mother the same way I took you."

"But it feels like I can fly!"

"Until a big truck comes along and clips your wing."

The boys doubled over in laughter, a little zonked after being in the truck for so many hours. "Okay boys, let's settle down." Preacher was uncharacteristically anxious, but couldn't get quiet with the Lord to figure out why because of all the commotion in the truck. He tapped his thumb on the top of the steering wheel, a sure sign he was deep in thought.

"Are we almost there?" Sammy asked.

"Huh? Uh, yes… We'll be there in about an hour."

"Bueno," said Juan Jose. "That gives us time to work on our plans for my papá. Do you have the notebook?"

Sammy nodded and pulled out the notebook full of the plans they'd been working on. They were convinced the reason Juan Jose's dad hadn't come home from the United States was because he was in some sort of danger, and they had made plans for every possible scenario they could think of so when they found him, they would know exactly what to do.

"Samuèl, there's something we have not considered. What if we find my papa, and he hasn't filled the hole in his heart? Will you help me tell him about Jesus?"

"Sure. But maybe he already knows."

"I don't think so. If he knew something so important, he would have told me and my mamá about it before he left."

When Gabriella approached the car, she wasn't sure Mona saw her. Her friend sat staring straight ahead and didn't flinch when Gabriella opened the passenger door. She knelt down beside her and put her hand on Mona's knee. "I'm sorry."

And then it came. The flood of anguish Mona had been holding in on the slight chance she'd been wrong, that Gabriella could somehow wake him up even though she hadn't been able to. But she hadn't. And now her friend was confirming it. Raul Alfonso Martinez Quiňones, the man she'd loved her entire life, was gone.

Mona fought against the cold hard steel thing that had crawled into the pit of her stomach. "No!" she wailed. "No! God, take it back. Please, please take it back."

Gabriella wrapped her arms around her, awkwardly because Mona sat so stiffly, and she tried to comfort her. "I'm sorry," she whispered. "I'm so, so sorry."

"I can't," cried Mona. "I can't. Can't."

"I know," Gabriella said, squeezing hard. "But we will."

The boys got tired of talking and planning the rescue, and they drifted off into a bumpy, sweaty road nap. Preacher used the quiet time to think and pray and seek the Lord about his anxiousness, and he came away with the feeling that he needed to get in touch with Gabriella. He pulled over at the first store he saw, which was a tienda in the front room of an old crumbling house. He talked the owner into letting him use the phone, but when he called Gabriella, the phone rang steadily. She must be out. But where could she be?

Mona remained in the car while the men carried the gurney up the porch stairs and wheeled it into the house. She sat there while Gabriella went inside with the men and made the arrangements for her Raul to be taken away. She dreaded the reappearance of the gurney, and closed her eyes when it appeared, weighed down with its burden, because she didn't want her last image of Raul to be of him on top of a gurney with a sheet covering his face. But when she heard the metal wheels crunch against the shell and sand drive, she reflexively opened her eyes. And then she began to scream.

After Preacher and the boys arrived in El Perdido, they hurriedly began to set up their makeshift stage in the main plaza which was located in the middle of town. The plaza was large, an obvious sign of the town's prosperity. The benches interspersed throughout were painted with bright colors that matched the colorful flags running up and down the light posts. Vendors sat on intricately woven blankets and hawked their handmade jewelry and baskets, while others pushed their carts, selling food and snacks to the hungry.

The boys were well rested from their nap, and although Juan Jose acted excited to be in a new place, Preacher noticed Sammy getting more and more subdued, seemingly withdrawing into himself.

The fire was starting to burn.

"Preacher," Juan Jose said. "What should I do now? How can I help?"

"We're finished for now," he said. "All we can do is sit back and watch God work through Sammy."

Sure enough, shortly after he'd spoken, Sammy walked onto the center of the stage. A small crowd had already gathered, curious to see what was happening. Sammy stood there, looking like the very young boy that he was, with his eyes closed and a serious expression on his face. He didn't seem to be in a hurry, and the crowd grew larger as more people came to see why this young gringo in purple Keds was standing on the stage.

Suddenly he opened his eyes and said softly. "Do you know you're going to live forever?"

"Live forever?" someone in the crowd shouted. "This kid's crazy."

"Yeah," said another. "Let's get out of here."

Sammy got louder. "What if I told you you weren't ever going to

152

die? That right now, in this very instant, you can choose the very place where you'll spend eternity?"

"Now I'm really leaving," said the heckler. "This kid's talking about religion."

"I would never promote religion," Sammy said loudly. "I hate religion. It takes more people to Hell than Satan himself."

The crowd grew quiet.

"What I'm talking about is getting to know the Creator of Heaven and Earth and deciding whether or not you want to serve Him. You see, God is an awesome God and he requires no one to call Him Lord against their will on this earth. But He does give us the opportunity.

"Do you really believe this is all there is?" he asked, spreading out his arms. "Do you long for a nice house, a good family, or a successful business? Will all of that truly satisfy you here?" he asked, thumping his chest. "In the secret places of your heart? Here's the deal," he said, pointing to the heckler. "You are going to die."

The crowd gasped and pulled back collectively. "As will you and you and you," he said pointing to various people in the crowd. "But what most people don't consider is this: you and you and you and all of us will surely live again. The question is where.

"You have been given the chance to know with certainty before you die what you will see when you open your eyes in the next life. Will it be a place of tremendous joy and celebration? Or will you, in the most important decision of your life, chose a place of utter destruction and despair? It's all up to you.

"Let me tell you a secret—religion won't get you where you want to go. It may get you a respected place in your community, pride for your good deeds, or a good reputation, but that's not what God wants from us.

"He wants our heart. Every last beat of it. He's not a God who will settle for a lukewarm heart. He's not a God who will accept fifty percent of you. No, He's a jealous God, a God who loves you with such a consuming passion He wants all of you. But Glory to God, He also gives us all His love in return.

"Now come, you who want this God for your own. Run, don't walk to the stage and lay down your life of selfishness and take on His cares and wants as your own. You are His glorious creation, and He knows His thoughts toward you. He has plans of good and not evil, of a future and a hope. Come. Come to the only one who can save you. Be sure if you die tonight, you'll be with the King in his Kingdom tomorrow."

For a moment it felt as if the crowd had swelled and was about to burst, and then everyone went silent and absolutely still. The heckler, the man who had put up such a fight, leapt onto the stage, walked over to Sammy and knelt down. "Tell me," he said. "What must I do to be saved?" Sammy knelt with him in prayer, and soon streams of people were filing onto the stage.

Preacher nudged Juan Jose. "Come on. Let's go on up."

"Up where?"

"To the stage. These people need to understand how to be saved."

"We'll, I sure can't tell them. I'll wait for you right here."

Preacher looked hard at Juan Jose, and then toward the crowd streaming onto the stage. "Son, how many people do you figure are waiting to hear God's word?"

"I don't know. Two hundred?"

"Hmm. Do you think Sammy and I can talk to them all by ourselves?"

"Preacher, I can't. I'm just a kid. I wouldn't even know what to say to them."

"We never do," he said, taking Juan Jose's arm and pulling him toward the stage. "He Himself puts the words in our mouths."

On stage, Sammy knelt with a family of five committing their lives to Christ. "What if I make a mistake?" the teenage girl asked.

"Ask God to forgive you and keep going."

"What if I'm not sure?" asked another.

Sammy turned and looked into the man's dark eyes. "Then you should pray and ask God to remove the deception that's blinding you."

"Will you pray with me?"

Sammy nodded and knelt down with the man. By the time they rose minutes later, the man's eyes shone with the light of Heaven.

"How can I thank you?" the man asked.

Sammy looked around at the people waiting to pray. He had been led by the Spirit to not give a call for group prayer tonight, but rather to pray individually with the people. Now he wondered if he had misunderstood.

"Help me pray with some of these people," he told the man.

"What? Me? I wouldn't know what to say."

"Don't worry, brother," he said before turning away to pray with another family. "God will give you the words."

After Gabriella talked to Mona and calmed her down some, she went back into the house. Her plan was to remove the things that would be difficult for Mona to see. She changed the bed linens, picked up Raul's scattered clothes and hung them in the closet, and then washed and put away the breakfast dishes.

Mona didn't move from the car.

After Gabriella tidied the house the best she could, she made some chamomile tea and carried it outside. She climbed into the driver's side of the car and put the wooden tray on the seat between them. Even with the car door open, the rich scent of tea and honey filled the small space. Mona didn't move. Gabriella looked out the front window and saw the sea had gone from a shimmery blue to a deep gray and was now taking on the bleak hues of the night. The sun had almost disappeared behind it, and she wondered if Mona had even noticed what would have been a spectacular sunset.

"I brought tea," she finally said, filling a cup and holding it out to her.

But Mona didn't take it, didn't even seem to register her presence. Gabriella took a sip of the tea and set it down on the tray. A mosquito flew in through the open door, its buzzing deafening in the silence. Gabriella watched it land on Mona's check. She didn't move to swat it away, so Gabriella reached over to brush it off, but Mona clasped on to her hand and held on. The mosquito had its fill and left quietly on its own.

"Why didn't God save him?" Mona whispered. "Is it because I refused to pray for him?"

"Oh honey, of course not."

"Then why?"

"I don't know," Gabriella admitted. "What I'm learning is sometimes He does things that make absolutely no sense to us."

"And that somehow makes you feel secure?"

Gabriella pursed her lips. "No. I don't know. Mona, look, I'm not an expert on God. I'm not even sure what I believe."

"I'm sorry. I didn't mean to be short with you."

Gabriella squeezed her hand in response. "It's okay. I know you didn't."

A flock of seagulls swooped down and gathered on the beach, their shadowy figures illuminated by the last rays of light put out by a fading sun. Another mosquito buzzed in, but Gabriella swatted it with her free hand.

"Do you want me to help you inside? I'll stay with you tonight, or if you'd prefer, you can come and stay with me for a while."

"I'm fine right here."

"Here? You mean in your house?"

Mona shook her head. "I think Raul tried to tell me he was going to die."

Gabriella mentally switched gears. "Do you want to tell me about it?"

"After Preacher and the boys left yesterday, Raul got very tired. He said something was heavy on his heart, and he needed to pray. I told him he was too sick to pray, that he had overextended himself all day and needed to rest. But he wouldn't listen to me. He stayed on his knees by the bed all afternoon until I finally insisted he get up and eat. He came to the kitchen and ate a little pozole, and then he went right back to his knees.

"Well, I'd had enough. I marched right into the bedroom and sat down on the bed next to him. When he looked up…" Mona swallowed hard, roughly brushed away a fresh wave of tears.

"It was so strange," she said in a hoarse whisper. "When he looked up from praying, he looked… I don't know how to explain it. It looked, well, like he'd been with someone who made him incredibly happy." She sat silent for a moment and let her tears fall freely. "It was the strangest thing I've ever seen. I'll never forget it."

"What happened then?"

Mona shook her head. "He pulled me down next to him, and I couldn't stop looking at his face. I just wanted to feel it, too. I wanted whatever it was he had experienced."

"'Mona,'" he said. "'Have I been a good esposo to you?'"

"What are you talking about?" I asked him. "You've been the best husband I could have ever hoped for."

"'This doesn't have to be the end,'" he said.

"The end of what?" I asked. "Raul, does your chest hurt now? Are you okay?"

He nodded and looked at me so lovingly. He said he was talking about when we die. That we could see each other in Heaven again. I stood up and told him he was being ridiculous. I reminded him the doctor said he just needed to rest.

"'The doctor doesn't know the end of things,'" he said.

"And you do?" I asked him.

He shook his head. "'Only God knows, esposa. But one day soon I will leave this earth and go to Heaven. And I'd like to know that when you die, you'll join me there.'"

I started to walk away, fussing about the dishes in the sink I needed to wash. But before I was out of the room, he called my name.

"Yes," I said, barely stopping to listen to what he had to say.

Mona's lips trembled as she remembered the scene. "He held up his Bible," she said. And then he told me there was something in it he wanted me to read.

"What is it, esposo?" I asked him. "What do I need to read?"

He smiled at me so sweetly. "'I don't know,'" he said. "'But promise me that when God shows it to you, you'll pay attention.'"

Mona reached down under the seat and pulled out a large, black Bible.

"Is that his—"

"—Yes, it's Raul's Bible." Mona lovingly ran her fingers over the edges of the pages. "I've been asking God all day what He wants me to see, what Raul was talking about, but He is so silent."

"No, He's not." Gabriella reached over and gently took the Bible, tears streaming down her face. "Mona, this is going to sound crazy, but I know what verse you're supposed to read. Let me tell you how it happened."

Raul's face lit up like a child's, and he turned to his Savior. "You did it! She'll be saved, won't she?"

"Did you doubt?"

"Yes, Lord," he shamefully admitted. His eyes widened, and before he could think about what he was doing, Raul lifted his arms and began moving gracefully to the glorious music always present in Heaven, giving himself over completely in dance to the honor of his King.

Chapter 17

The crowd had thinned out, and everyone who stayed to help was now praying with the few remaining people. "What do you mean you're not sure you're ready?" asked Juan Jose, shaking his head in bewilderment. "You mean you want to live in the lake of fire? You think it gets hot here in the summer? That's nothing compared to Hell! And the people there don't even have a winter!"

"Um, Juan Jose?" said Preacher. "Why don't you let me finish talking to this young woman and you can start tearing down the stage."

"Okay." He walked to the other side of the stage and joined Sammy and the stranger. "Preacher said we should tear down the stage."

"Sure," said Sammy. "But it's days like this I miss my crate. I could just pick it up and carry it away."

"Tired?" asked the new believer. "Here, let me help. We'll have it torn down in no time."

They had just loaded the last of the wood in the truck when Preacher left the woman and walked over. "Good work, boys." He looked at the man. "I thank you for your help, too."

He shrugged. "I figure I owe you my life. Literally." He smiled. "Will you stay in town tonight?"

Preacher looked at the night sky and the two exhausted boys. "Yes, I believe we will. Then we'll leave first thing in the morning. Where's a good place around here to get a room?"

"I would be honored if you would stay at my house. We'll feed you a good meal and there's plenty of room for everyone."

"Thank you for your kindness, but I'd hate to impose."

"If I were being completely honest, I'd have to admit my motives aren't entirely pure."

"Oh?"

He shook his head. "You see, my wife Herlinda needs to hear your message, and I think she'd take it better from you than me. She's had a difficult past and is generally skeptical about religion." He glanced quickly at Sammy. "Excuse me, I mean the things of God."

"Herlinda, huh? She didn't originally come from the town of Rendición did she?"

The man looked surprised. "Yes, but how could you possibly know that?"

Preacher laughed his deep, belly laugh. "Because," he said, "there are absolutely no coincidences with God."

Hector Mendez pulled his shiny, new black car up to Juan Jose's house and shut off the engine. The tick-tock of the cooling engine irritated the man. He hated to make house calls. How difficult is it to make your rent payments on time, anyway? Sure, her husband had disappeared, along with many other men who went to the U.S. to try and earn some money, but it wasn't his problem. Instead of sitting around and waiting for him to return, she should do something to earn some money. He simply had no patience for people who refused to pay their own way.

Well, he would collect from her right now. Who did she think she was, anyway? Holding out on him? She shouldn't have agreed to rent the place if she didn't intend to make the payments.

He stepped out of the car, aggravated because his shoes and pant cuffs would be covered with a fine dusting of sand by the time he left. He glanced to the right and saw the new wood on the chicken coop and felt his anger build. *Is that what she did with her money instead of paying rent?* He advanced to the house and rapped loudly on the door.

Juan Jose's mom came to the door, wiping her hands on her apron. "Hola Señor. How are you?"

He ignored the greeting and began reading the notice in his hands. "Rosa, I'm here to inform you that you are currently three months behind on your rent and this is the bank's formal and final notice. Unless the entire balance is paid within seven days, you and your family will be evicted."

Rosa opened the door and stepped out on the porch. "Hector Mendez, shame on you," she said in Spanish. "If your mother were still alive, she'd be heartbroken."

"I'm afraid evoking my dead mother's spirit won't help you this time. We've talked about this before, Rosa. The bank simply cannot afford to carry you on this anymore."

"But, my husband hasn't yet returned. I'm sure he'll be back any day now, and then he'll straighten everything out."

Hector shifted impatiently to his other foot. "How long has Rodolfo been gone?"

Rosa looked at her feet and quietly said, "Three years."

"Have you heard from him in all that time?"

"You know I haven't," she said, the embarrassment muffling her voice.

"People do things we'd never imagine once they see the abundance and free living in the United States. Although, I must admit I'm a little more than shocked at Rodolfo's abandonment of his family. I would have never expected it."

Rosa looked up sharply. "He has not abandoned us. He would have come home or contacted us unless something is preventing him from doing it."

Hector let out a bored sigh. "I'm sure believing that makes you feel better, but the truth is he left you with no way to support yourself. And unless you're caught up on your rent within a week, the bank will take possession of the property. You've been notified, Rosa." He turned and started toward his car.

Rosa felt overwhelmed at her helplessness at the hands of this cruel man, and everything in her wanted to strike back. "You're not the one to talk about being abandoned, are you?" she called after him.

But Hector kept walking as if she and Rodolfo and Juan Jose and the life they'd built in this very home didn't matter. She wanted to tell him she knew he wasn't everything he pretended to be. "Does it make you feel better to let everyone believe Herlinda died?" she yelled in desperation.

Hector stopped and absorbed the information, keeping his back to her.

"I guess it's better for your precious reputation than telling people she divorced you and moved to El Perdido."

Hector stayed perfectly still for a beat or two more and then continued walking to his car. If Rosa could have seen his face, she would have been horrified at the thin, insidious smirk spreading across it.

Gabriella told Mona about the Bible study she'd had with Sammy that morning, and how she felt led to tell her about the verse they'd studied. Mona was all ears, hungry for anything that could give her an instant of peace. So Gabriella picked up Raul's Bible and read the verse. When Mona didn't react, she tried to explain it. "Don't you understand, Mona? This says Raul didn't die. He still lives. Only now he lives in Heaven instead of here."

Mona nodded slightly. "Leave me be."

Confused, Gabriella asked, "Do you want me to help you inside?"

"Go on back to your own house, now," she said softly. "I'll be all right."

But she hadn't gone home. Instead, Gabriella slipped quietly out of the car, taking the tea with her, and went inside Mona's house. She fixed a small dinner and took a sandwich to the car. When Mona didn't acknowledge her, she noiselessly left it on the seat and returned to the house.

Then she sat in the living room looking out the window and worrying. Mona hadn't budged. From the window, Gabriella watched her friend stare out the front windshield and stare at the night sea.

Hector slammed down the phone. There was no reason for the man to be so rude. *I've always taken care of things, why would he believe this time would be any different?* He walked out of the building, careful to lock the door behind him, and hurried to his car. Once inside, he gunned the engine and pointed the car south. Finally, there would no longer be any loose ends.

Although she didn't say so, Herlinda seemed to recognize Preacher immediately. He guessed she remembered him from the old days in Rendiciòn because during that time, he had tried to befriend her husband in an attempt to gain insight into the tanker situation. Preacher noticed how she tried to keep her face angled away from him, letting her shoulder length black hair wisp over her face. She was polite enough, efficiently putting together a tasty meal of pan fried enchiladas served with beans and rice, and for desert, a homemade lime sherbet she had fortuitously made that morning. But underneath the good manners and capable hospitality, Preacher sensed a deep fear. He wondered if her unease had anything to do with Hector telling everyone she was dead. He needed to speak with her alone to find out what was going on. And why Hector had lied about her.

Preacher pushed away from the table. "That was the best meal I've had in recent memory. Gracias Senora."

"Yes," said Sammy. "I'm stuffed. Thank you, Senora."

"It was my pleasure," she said.

"Si Senora," Juan Jose burst out in his typical fast talking manner. "I'd ask for another serving of that delicious ice cream, but my mamá told me it's rude to ask for seconds in someone else's house. But it sure was good." Suddenly, he reached down and grabbed his leg. "Aye! Samuél, why did you kick me?"

Ernesto laughed. "Juan Jose, I have to agree with you. The ice cream was excellent. I'm going to have another bowl. Anyone else?"

"Yes!" The two boys yelled in unison.

"Good," said Ernesto, winking at Preacher. "I'd hate to have to eat it all alone."

When he got up to go to the kitchen, Preacher said, "Why don't you boys follow him with your bowls to make it easier for him?"

The two boys scrambled after him, and after they'd left the room, Preacher leaned over the table. "Senora," he said quietly. "Please don't be afraid. But it's important that I speak to you."

Herlinda shook her head. "My husband. He knows nothing about that part of my life."

"Well, I'll be." He sat back and thought for a moment. "Your husband wants me to talk to you about God," he said thoughtfully. "I suppose if we talked about both things, it wouldn't be untruthful."

Herlinda nodded, looking resigned. "I've always feared my past would eventually catch up with me." She looked up suddenly, her eyes wide with fear. "How did you find me? Hector doesn't know where I am, does he?"

"No Senora. But I do have some questions about Hector. He's told people for years that you're dead. Why would he do that?"

She shook her head and lowered her voice. "I know things that could get him in a lot of trouble. At one point, I became afraid of him and left, and I've been hiding from him ever since." She looked intently at Preacher. "I believe my life would be in danger if he could find me. Are you sure he doesn't know where I am?"

Preacher shook his head. "No, I learned your whereabouts from Rosa, the mother of Juan Jose." He tilted his head toward the kitchen. "The boy's father, Rodolfo, left your name and address buried in his yard, and we recently found it. I'm guessing Rodolfo suspected he might not make it back from the U.S. and did it as some sort of insurance."

"So, he hasn't returned then."

Preacher shook his head.

She nodded, taking in the information. "And you're sure Rosa wouldn't tell Hector where to find me?"

"I'm sure."

Her shoulders fell as the tension she'd been holding eased. "Well," she said rising. "I guess we'd better get this over with."

Ernesto came back into the room with the two boys happily trailing after him. "More anyone?" he asked, holding up the almost empty plastic ice cream container.

THE FRAGRANCE OF SURRENDER

"No. Preacher and I are going to the back porch to talk."

"Good," he said, winking at Preacher. "That leaves all the more for us."

Once they settled into the large patio chairs, Herlinda turned to Preacher. "Before we begin, you should know I'm not even remotely interested in your religion."

Preacher nodded. "Okay. But are you aware your husband gave his life to Christ tonight?"

She pinched her lips together and shook her head. "He doesn't have the same past that I do."

Preacher leaned forward, his elbows on his knees. "Senora, in the eyes of the Lord, your past doesn't matter. When we come to Him in true repentance all our past is washed away. We're made new."

She smiled tightly. "We'll see if you feel the same way after you hear my story."

Preacher nodded, his silence encouraging her to go on.

She took a deep breath and blew it out slowly. "I wish I could tell you I was innocent in the things that went on, but it would be a lie." She looked him directly in the eyes. "I played a large role in what happened." She closed her eyes and looked away. "But I never intended for it to go as far as it did."

Once again, Preacher nodded.

"It all started many years ago, when the oil companies began talking about using our port to dock their tankers."

"Yes, I remember the fighting well."

She nodded. "Publically, the fight centered on how the tankers would affect the town morally and financially. The people in favor of the tankers were convinced the new docks would enable the town to grow and prosper, while the opponents feared the sailors would bring immorality and destroy the family atmosphere of the village. But that's only how things appeared on the surface. In reality, the struggle was about much, much more."

"Oh?"

She nodded. "What no one knows is that the village is sitting on a fortune. There are silver veins running for miles and miles directly underneath it."

"Silver?"

Herlinda nodded. "Quite literally a fortune without measure."

"I don't understand. How does this relate to the tankers?"

"When the tanker companies first announced their intentions to make Rendiciòn a port city, no one was happy about it, including us. We realized the village would undergo massive changes, and we wanted things to stay as they were. And although we didn't protest it publically, we certainly didn't support it."

"But I thought you did. Everyone heard about Hector's opposition to the Juarez's protests."

"Yes, but that didn't occur until after the fire."

"The fire in the Juarez's orange grove?"

"Yes, it wasn't until the aftermath of the fire that we learned of the silver. And it was the reason we began campaigning so hard for the tankers."

"We?"

She shook her head. "I'll get to that in a minute. You see, the problem was most of the silver deposits ran under private property, and the owners of those properties legally had the rights to the silver."

"But you wanted it."

She lowered her eyes. "Yes. And the tankers gave us the perfect opportunity to begin the process of taking the land."

"I'm still missing the connection."

"Rendiciòn has always been an ideal place to live, and the families who lived there had done so for generations. But after the announcement that the town would be turned into a port city, people began talking about selling their properties and relocating rather than living in that type of environment. The protestors did an excellent job of documenting the decline of other villages that had welcomed the tankers."

"So you campaigned for the tankers, not to prosper the village, but to force people to sell so you could buy their properties."

She nodded.

"And when the protestors drove the tankers to another port?"

"We had to change our tactics. You see, we still wanted the properties, but now the people had no reason to sell."

Preacher nodded, as if he finally understood. "So, you created one. A financial crisis."

"Yes. The people involved in our little group were the pillars of our community. The mayor and the police chief were involved as well as some other high ranking village officials. They controlled the jobs, the taxes, the land values—"

"—and the loans?"

She nodded. "Yes, because Hector and I owned the bank, we were in a position to deny loans to the families who owned the land we wanted. And after the jobs dried up and taxes were raised so high they couldn't possibly pay them, people became desperate enough to do anything in return for a loan."

"Is that when you introduced them to the coyotes?"

She nodded slowly. "And that's when the plan took a detour."

"Go on."

"The idea was to ask the families to take out loans using their land as collateral. We convinced the men to go with the coyotes so they could find a job in the U.S., which would enable them to make their loan payments. The plan was to foreclose on the properties before the men came home. We would own the land, but lease it back to the families until we'd moved on all the properties we wanted. And then we would simply kick them out and drill for the silver."

"But the men never came home."

"No."

"Why not? What happened to them?"

She shook her head. "I'm not sure. The coyotes were told to make sure the men were detained in the U.S. for as long as possible. They were told to track them and as soon as the men were settled and able to send money home, report them to immigration. That way, they'd be deported and arrive back here with nothing to show for their efforts. We'd own their land and collect what we could from them in rent until we were ready to begin mining for the silver. At that point, we would terminate the leases." She looked up sharply. "Have they started? Have they already drilled for the silver?"

Preacher shook his head. "I don't think so, no. There are many people who still rent their properties from the bank."

She nodded. "I wonder what's keeping them from moving forward."

Preacher studied her closely. Her eyes and jawline had softened over the years and she had the look of a typical aging woman whose world revolved around grandkids. But listening to her made him realize she was not at all a typical woman. When he thought of what she'd been a part of, he was stunned at the coldness of it. He shook off the shiver crawling up his spine, and asked another question, hoping to find out once and for all what had happened. "So you don't know what happened to the men? Juan Jose's father isn't the only man who didn't make it back."

She shook her head. "That's what Rodolfo was trying to find out."

"I don't understand."

"I became very concerned about the men who weren't coming back, and when I brought it up at one of our meetings, I was told to stay out of it. The others told me that if I wanted my share of the fortune, I should keep quiet and not ask questions." She slowly shook her head. "But I couldn't. I didn't know what was happening to the men, but I didn't believe they had abandoned their families." Her eyes begged Preacher to understand. "I knew these men. And while the role I played in taking away their properties is unforgivable, I would have never agreed to a plan where they would be harmed. But as far as I could tell, something very bad was happening to them. And the fact that the group, including Hector, had shut me out made me concerned for my own safety.

"So I planned my escape. I wanted to divorce Hector and leave, but I needed to do as much as I could in secret so he wouldn't be alerted. I went to a neighboring town to file for divorce, and when the time came for Hector to be involved in the process, I left him a note, telling him if he granted me the divorce, I would disappear and his secrets would be safe.

"I know what I did was cowardly." She looked at Preacher, her eyes willing him to understand. "But I was sure the group would never let me leave alive because I knew too much and there was so much money at stake. But right before I left, I saw the paperwork for a new loan." She tilted her head toward the house. "It was Juan Jose's dad, Rodolfo. I guess in some small way, what I did next was my attempt to make up for my sins."

"You warned him?"

"Yes, but by then the loan had gone through and the bank owned the land as collateral for a loan he couldn't possibly repay. After I explained the situation to him, Rodolfo said he had to at least try to get a job in the U.S. so he could save his family's land. He believed that because he understood the dangers, he could find a way to avoid them. But it looks like he was wrong."

Preacher shook his head. "So the men may not be alive."

"That's my guess." She glanced at the house. "He seems like a fine boy. I despise my role in his pain."

"He misses his father. Every day he wonders if this will be the day he comes home."

She closed her eyes and nodded.

"How did Rodolfo get your address?"

She shrugged. "Before I left town, I gave it to him and asked him to contact me if he found out what happened to the other men."

Preacher nodded thoughtfully. "Herlinda, there's something else I need to ask you."

She reluctantly nodded, her dull eyes filled with pain.

"The other boy, Samuél. He's the grandchild of Ignacio and Maria Juarez. Do you recognize the name?"

"Oh God," she said, burying her head in her hands. "What have I done?"

Chapter 18

The morning sun nudged Gabriella, and she woke up stiff from sleeping in the chair all night. She looked out the window, hoping Mona had come in during the night, and was disappointed to find her in the car still staring out the front windshield. *God, what do I do?*

She stood up, stretched her cramped legs, and went to the kitchen to make coffee. Surely Mona would want some after such a long night.

A few minutes later, she made her way across the yard with the little wooden tray. When she opened the car door, the scent of fresh laundry came rushing out. It smelled as if something had been washed clean. Made brand new.

Mona turned toward her, her eyes lit up like the morning sky. "Why did you bring the coffee out here?" she asked. "Why don't we go into the casa? We have many things to do."

Hector relaxed once he saw the road sign welcoming him to El Perdido. He chided himself yet again for not knowing that his ex-wife had been living only a few hours away. He had been humiliated when she left him so many years ago, and instead of living with the shame, he told people in the village she'd died while visiting her family across the state. After all, he couldn't explain the real reason why she was no longer in town. He had granted her the secret divorce in hopes of using the proceedings to find her, but she'd been smart, and he'd been unable to pinpoint her location.

And now there was no way he was going to let her weakness keep him from the fortune that lie underneath the ground. He'd been forced to tell the men in the group the truth about her disappearance, because as long as she was alive they couldn't possibly begin drilling for the silver. It would draw too much attention, and they were afraid Herlinda would come forward and expose them for what they'd done. In fact, before she left years ago, they had considered silencing her because her concern for the missing men was making them nervous.

And so they waited to drill. For decades. But all he had to do now was find her and deal with the situation, and he and the remaining men could finally collect their fortune. He decided to tell people around town he was her brother and they'd lost contact with each other. And when someone took pity on him and told him where to find his long lost sister, he'd go to her. And then he'd make sure she never told the story. Then they could begin drilling for what they'd worked so hard for.

With daybreak came crushing waves of sadness that seemed to overwhelm Herlinda to the point of breaking. Preacher comforted her the best he could. He was stunned at the story she'd told him. While her role in the scheme was bad enough, he took heart that at least she didn't have anything to do with the fate of the missing men. *Lord,* he prayed silently. *You would have her come to repentance as well.*

"I need you to come back to Rendición with me," he said "I think Gabriella deserves to hear this from you."

"What about Hector?"

"Since the authorities will have to be notified, we can make some calls and ask that Hector is detained before we arrive."

She nodded, finally yielding to the fate she'd tried so desperately to avoid. "Give me a minute with my husband." she said quietly. "And I'll be ready to go."

Hector couldn't believe his luck. Someone at the very first store he'd stopped at told him exactly where to find Herlinda. When he learned she had remarried, Hector felt an intense agitation rise up inside of him. *How dare she go on with her life and leave us in limbo waiting for the chance to claim what we've worked so hard for?* A husband would also put a kink in his plans. In order to silence her, he needed to take her someplace isolated and it would be more difficult to persuade her to go with him if her husband was around. Unless she'd told her husband about the things they'd done. Then he'd have to silence the both of them.

He looked at his watch. He would know soon enough how difficult it would be. According to the man at the store, she lived right around the corner.

As Herlinda spoke in urgent whispers to Ernesto, Preacher called the authorities in Rendición and told them what he'd heard. He was relieved when they agreed to pick up Hector and detain him, along with the other men Herlinda named as being part of the scheme. The policeman agreed to wait for a call from Preacher before taking Herlinda into custody. Gabriella would need some time to talk to the woman about her parents.

Next, Preacher woke up the boys, gave them breakfast and loaded them into the truck. They immediately fell asleep again, their heads leaning against the hard seat back. He was in a hurry to get back to Rendición, but Herlinda was still filling in Ernesto on their plans. He looked at his watch again.

"We'll follow behind you."

Startled, Preacher turned around to find Ernesto, his face full of anxiety. "I need to hear her story. But I figure we'll have plenty of time to talk on the road."

Preacher nodded. "I understand, brother. I'll be careful not to lose you, but if I do, Herlinda knows the way."

They finished loading their cars, pulled out of the drive and started on the road that would lead them back home.

Gabriella and Mona stood side by side in the kitchen making chorizo and eggs and orange blossom water. Gabriella looked up from the frying pan to find Mona staring out the kitchen window, tears streaming down her face.

"I'm sorry," Mona said softly.

"You're sorry? For what?"

"For taking your pain so lightly." She raised the dishrag to her face and coarsely wiped away the tears. "I didn't know hurt like this existed. How did you ever survive it?"

Gabriella reached over and squeezed her hand. "No one can understand that kind of pain unless they've felt it."

"Part of me still doesn't believe it. I keep thinking Raul is just in the next room." She shrugged and looked bewildered. "I have the strongest urge to fix him breakfast."

"I'm sorry. I wish I could take away your pain."

She nodded and wiped her eyes again. "Do you believe it? The verse you showed me yesterday?"

Gabriella hesitated. "Honestly? I don't know. But I want to. I really do."

"I do. Nothing else makes sense. Raul was too good of a man to simply disappear into nothingness." She fussed with dishrag, wiping away an imaginary spot on the countertop. "Besides, Raul was the smartest man I've ever known. If he says we must know this God to see each other again in Heaven, then it must be true."

"So..." Gabriella said, shutting off the flame and removing the pan. "You're a believer?"

Mona put down the rag and took a ragged breath. "Yes, I guess I am."

And once again, Raul worshiped his King.

Hector pulled up to the address the man at the store had given him and turned off the engine. He noticed with envy the wide front porch and the colorful potted flowers lining the rails. *Looks like she's made a life for herself,* he thought. *Did she really believe she could hide from me forever?*

He got out of the car and walked to the front door. He'd decided on the drive up that the direct approach was the best way to deal with the situation. She'd gotten the best of him during the divorce, but this time he wouldn't let her win. Gratefully, he felt the hard pistol in his jacket pocket. He wasn't as strong as he used to be, and since he might have to deal with Herlinda's husband, a gun might come in handy.

After knocking on the door, he was met by an irritating silence. He knocked again, a little harder this time, and while he waited he looked around. The wicker furniture on the porch was showing signs of wear, and the paint was beginning to peel off the railings. *Stupid woman,* he thought. *She could have had all the money she needed if she hadn't developed a sudden conscience.* It had been so long since they'd first discovered the silver that some members of the group had died, and those that remained were as old as he was. He took out his frustrations on the door and knocked even harder than before.

"They're not home," said a voice from behind him.

Hector turned to find an older woman standing on the porch behind him. "I saw Herlinda and Ernesto leave about ten minutes ago with another man and two boys. Can I give her a message for you?"

"No thank you, Senora. Any idea where they were going?"

The woman shook her head.

Hector asked for a description of the man, and when she described him as very large with wild grayish hair, he instantly thought of Preacher. Suddenly, his errand took on a new urgency. If Preacher was involved, it probably meant he was trying to convince Herlinda to do the right thing. And that meant exposing him and the other men.

He jumped in this car and took off towards home. He would have to get to Herlinda and everyone else in the group before they reached Rendiciòn. Otherwise, they would ruin everything he'd worked for.

Hours later, Preacher, the two boys, Herlinda and Ernesto pulled up in front of Mona's house. They had gone to Gabriella's house first, and when they realized she wasn't home, they took the chance that she'd be here. Of course, they had no idea why.

Sammy and Juan Jose bounded up the porch steps. "Raul! Raul! Juan Jose is now a preacher, too!"

They found the women at the back of the property, sweaty and dirty. They were digging a very large hole.

"Mom! What are you doing? And where's Raul?" The women looked at each other, neither of them wanting to break the boy's hearts. Then they noticed Preacher and two strangers walking towards them.

"Gabriella," Preacher said, once they'd reached them. "I brought someone you need to talk to." He glanced at the large hole in the ground and the dirt that covered the women. "My sweet Jesus," he said softly. He looked at Mona for confirmation and closed his eyes when he saw her tears. "Lord," he said under his breath. "We trust You in all things." His big hands gently reached for Gabriella's shovel, and he motioned her towards Herlinda. "Go on in the house," he said. "This woman has a story you need to hear."

She handed him the shovel, all the while staring at Herlinda. "I know you," she said. "I was only a child, but I'll never forget your face."

Herlinda nodded. "Will you speak to me?"

"Will I? I've been waiting to talk to you my entire life."

Hector's palms were sweating as he drove down the long drive leading to Gabriella's house. He had heard that Preacher traveled with her son, so he assumed they would come here to drop the boy off before he and Herlinda did whatever they came to do. He figured it would be the best chance he'd have of stopping their plans.

But what he didn't expect was the police car that suddenly came up behind him, cutting him off from an exit. He panicked for a moment, but then he remembered who the members of his group were. They had all, in their day, run this pathetic little village. In fact, he'd given a loan to this policeman's brother just last month to buy a house. He stopped his car and got out, only because the policeman blocked his way and didn't give him an option.

"Is there a problem?" he asked.

"Yes, Mr. Mendez. I'm afraid I'm going to have to take you to the station for some questions."

"About what?"

The officer shook his head. "We'll have to get it all straightened out at the station,"

"I'm afraid I don't have time for that," he said. "Why don't you ask me your questions here?"

"Can't do that. Come on over here and climb in."

"To what? Your police car? I don't think so."

The officer made a call on his radio and released a pair of handcuffs from his belt. "I'm not asking you, sir. I need you to get in the car. Now."

Hector stood still. "Does Chief Fernandez know about this? I'm sure he wouldn't approve."

"You mean the old chief? I'm afraid he doesn't have a say in the police department anymore." The man turned Hector around and put the cuffs on this hands.

"This is an outrage! You're going to regret this. I have friends who can make your life miserable."

"You'll have a chance to talk to them about it at the station," he said. "They've all been picked up and are there now. Let's just get in the car, okay?"

Hector allowed the man to steer him towards the patrol car and settle him into the backseat. He wouldn't go down easily, he decided. And he would make Herlinda pay. Somehow, he would make her regret the day she crossed him.

Back at Mona's house, Preacher watched Gabriella and Herlinda walk away, and then he turned to Mona. "Why here?" he asked, indicating the hole.

She shrugged. "We've never been apart, not for more than a day." She looked toward the house. "I'd just feel better with him near me."

He nodded. "I understand."

"I know about the note you left Gabriella's parents," she said. "Raul believed in you, but I have my doubts."

He began shoveling dirt out of the hole and piling it up next to it. "Raul and I spoke about the note before he died, and he came to understand why I left it." He looked at her and softened his voice. "I'm not the person who harmed them, Mona. That person is inside with Gabriella, and the police are on the way here to arrest her."

"That couple hurt the Juarezes?"

He shook his head. "It was the woman and some other people from the village. The man is her husband, and he just learned about all this today." They looked toward the house and saw Ernesto standing outside the door waiting for Gabriella and Herlinda to finish their conversation.

"Is Gabriella safe with her?"

He nodded. "Yes, the woman has done some horrible things, but I don't believe she poses any threat now. In her own way, she tried to make up for her sins by getting Gabriella to safety all those years ago, and also by trying to warn Rodolfo." He shook his head. "I'm sure Gabriella is safe with her." He stopped shoveling and leaned on the handle. "After the police come and the boys are in bed, can we talk? I'd like to make things right between us. Raul would want that."

She nodded. Anything for her Raul.

"But what I don't understand," he said, beginning to shovel the dirt again. "Is how you ended up with the note instead of the Juarezes."

She shrugged. "I always assumed they got it. You mean they didn't?"

"I don't believe so, no. They never came to meet me that night."

She nodded thoughtfully. "Shortly after their disappearance, I went back to put things in order and check on the house. I didn't know where they went, but at the time I never imagined they would be gone for so long." She glanced at the house. "Of course, I believed that wherever they were, Gabriella was with them. So I cleaned and straightened the house, and then I went to the porch to sweep away all the sand that had collected there. That's when I found the note. It was underneath the rocker in the corner of the porch."

"The wind must have blown it away," Preacher said.

"I guess so." She shook her head in disbelief. "Imagine, for all those years I believed you dragged them away and harmed them. It's why I didn't believe what Raul tried to tell me about God."

"I was trying to warn them," he said gently. "And if the wind hadn't blown away the note, they would probably still be alive."

Mona dropped her shovel. "I guess I owe you an apology."

"It's not necessary," he said. "I would have come to same conclusion. But Mona," he hesitated. "Why didn't you go to the police about the note?"

"I did," she said. "The police chief told me I was meddling and I should just let them do their jobs." She looked down and kicked the dirt. "I wanted to talk to Raul about it, but he was so distraught about the Juarezes. And as time went on—" She looked at him and shrugged. "I just didn't know what to do."

"That makes sense," he nodded. "The woman inside said the police chief was in on the scheme."

They continued digging in silence for a while, and then Preacher spoke again. "Mona, I feel like I would be letting Raul down if I didn't talk to you about something. Do you understand that although Raul is no longer on this earth, he is still alive?"

Mona smiled broadly and nodded. "Yes Preacher, I've come to understand a lot of things since I last saw you. And I will see him again in Heaven."

"Well, I'll be," he said. "I imagine Raul is dancing with delight in Heaven as we speak."

Sammy and Juan Jose ran over and wanted to know why they were digging such a big hole. Preacher turned his attention toward them and told them he had something they needed to talk about. The three of them made their way towards an old tree that stood alone in the yard.

Gabriella and Herlinda settled down in the living room with two glasses of cold ice tea. Herlinda was nervous at first and kept looking at the door as if someone would come in and save her from what she had to do.

Gabriella's stomach swirled and her hands shook as she brought the glass of tea to her lips. Although it had been years since she last saw her, just sitting in the same room as Herlinda caused her to relive that awful night from so many years ago. She once again felt the panic and confusion she had as a child. Her stomach churned violently and a familiar aching filled her throat. *What will she tell me?* she wondered. Now that she was on the verge of having the answers she'd always longed for, she was afraid to learn the truth.

"Preacher said you've been seeking answers about your parents for years. I know what happened to them, and if you'd like, I'll tell you what I know."

Gabriella nodded, unable to speak.

"I need to start earlier, before your parents. It's the only way things will make sense to you."

"Go on."

Herlinda nodded and drew in a deep breath. She was nervous to tell Gabriella the truth, but once she started speaking, the words wouldn't stop and the more she spoke the easier it became. Within an hour, she'd told Gabriella almost everything she'd told Preacher the night before.

Gabriella sat back in her chair, shocked by what she'd heard. A mass of fragmented emotions rocked her insides.

"For money?" she whispered. "You did all this for money?"

Herlinda lowered her eyes and nodded.

"But all the families you hurt. The lives that were lost." She suddenly sat up straighter. "Look at me," she said.

Reluctantly, Herlinda raised her eyes to meet Gabriella's.

"Do you know what it feels like to lose someone you love? Don't you understand that it takes away a piece of who you are that you can never get back? It changes you in a way that..." She blew out her breath and tried to contain her emotions. "That one moment," she started. "That instant when you realize you've seen the person you love for the very last time, you're never the same after that. Everything changes in that moment, and..." She sighed, her breath shaking with frustration. "Don't you understand? There's no going back from there. It can't be undone"

I'm sorry. I wish I had been a stronger woman."

Gabriella wanted to walk away from her, this woman who had so callously taken from so many people, but the next question, the obvious one, hung in the air between them, weighty as a jury verdict seconds before it's pronounced. She couldn't wait any longer to hear about the elusive mystery that had haunted her for her entire life. "My parents," she said. "What happened to them?"

Herlinda lowered her eyes again and nodded, confirming to herself she was doing the right thing by telling Gabriella the truth. "I'm afraid I'm also responsible for their deaths."

Gabriella closed her eyes and went still. Although it went against all reason, she'd always held on to the hope that maybe, just maybe, they were still alive. And now the knowledge that they weren't sliced through her heart. "You killed them?" she asked in disbelief.

Herlinda shook her head quickly. "No. But I could have saved them, and I chose not to."

"Tell me. My entire life I've needed to understand why my parents never came back for me."

"Do you remember when your parent's orange grove was burned?"

"Yes. There were rumors your husband did it in retaliation for my father's protests of the tankers."

She shook her head. "He didn't. I believe that fire was set by someone who was upset by your parent's activities, but it's what happened after the fire that matters."

"Go on."

"You see, when the ground was burned so badly, it exposed an unusual rock layer, and your father wasn't sure if the land was still suitable for planting. So he hired a geologist to examine the burned ground and determine whether an orange grove would still be viable there. When the geologist examined the newly exposed rock, he discovered large amounts of galena, which is a lead ore that contains high amounts of silver."

"Oh," cried Gabriella. "He discovered silver on our land?"

Herlinda nodded. "Yes, but that was only the beginning. Hector and I contacted the geologist and asked him to perform an analysis on other areas of the village, and he found large quantities of galena all over the place. We eventually had the rocks tested and analyzed at a deeper level, and we discovered that deep silver veins run underneath the entire village."

"My God," said Gabriella. "My parents were killed because of what they knew?"

"I'm afraid so." She set down her empty glass of tea. "When I heard about the plans to make them disappear that night, I stayed quiet. In retrospect, of course, I wish I had warned them, but... well, I didn't." She shook her head. "When the men came home, proud that they had pushed your parents off a cliff—"

"—Excuse me," Gabriella said. "My parents died by being shoved off a cliff?"

"Yes."

She closed her eyes, and felt for a moment the utter terror her parents must have felt on that night. *My God, give me the strength to hear the rest of this.* "Which cliff did they fall over?"

Herlinda shrugged. "I'm not sure. Somewhere around their home, I think."

Gabriella shook her head in disbelief, finally understanding why she'd been so drawn to the cliff by her house.

"Anyway, I couldn't get you off my mind. The men hadn't realized there was a child in the house. If they had, you probably would have been drowned that day, too."

"Why did you wait two days to come for me? I was just a child and scared to death."

"I needed to wait until they were occupied with something else so they wouldn't get suspicious. As crazy as it sounds, I was obsessed with saving your life. The guilt for not speaking up in time to save your parents was enormous. And so I saved you instead."

"And you've just lived with this knowledge your entire life? Of lives being ruined and people being murdered? How is it possible that you haven't come forward with this information before now?"

"You don't understand, there was no one to go to. Everyone in authority was in on the scheme. And besides," she shrugged slightly. "I was afraid for my own life. I knew the men in the group would kill me if I exposed them."

Gabriella stared at the woman who was responsible for taking away her parents, her childhood, and her chance of a life without unrelenting pain, and she felt nothing but an aching pity. What must it be like to be so driven by greed, to be so willing to sacrifice other people's lives for your own? It struck her that despite the life of pain she'd led, she wouldn't trade places with Herlinda for anything. She wondered what kind of demons the woman wrestled with each night as she laid in bed. Or even worse, maybe she didn't struggle at all.

No, she'd much rather have her messed up emotions, regrets and unfulfilled wishes than the life of the woman who sat across from her. She had loved, and although she'd lost it, she knew what it felt like to be loved back. And now she wanted to love her friends and family in the way she'd always longed to be loved herself. She would. She'd be the best mom and friend she could.

Gabriella sat still, unsure how to go forward, take the next step. "What happens now?" she asked.

"The police will arrest me. As I understand it, they've already picked up Hector and the other men. They should be here any minute."

Gabriella stood. "Thank you for telling me this," she said. "Now, I need to go and be with my son."

When she walked out the back door, she was confronted with yet another emotional scene. Preacher held the two boys tightly as they grieved for their friend.

And so she began to run. She ran from the past, and everything that had bound her for her entire life. She vowed to free herself from the chains that had held her down for so long. *Oh God*, she prayed, *I want to live my life without being so afraid of everything. I want to love without the fear of loss, to wake up every day and not dread what could come. I desperately want to be the kind of mother Sammy deserves.*

At the same time, she ran toward the future, this crazy life where she would love her son while trusting him to God. She would feel things and not stuff her emotions every time they came to the surface. She would mourn her parents, Nicolas, and she realized in a moment of clarity that it was possible to experience that pain and not die. She would find out who she was, maybe for the first time in her life, and live the life she was born to live. Yes, she decided as she wildly raced toward the devastating scene before her, she would learn to trust this unpredictable God, who had somehow used these seemingly unrelated circumstances to bring her life full circle. They were burying Raul, but with hope. This wasn't the end, she knew it in the depths of her soul. He would live again.

When she heard Sammy sob, she stopped and saw in him what she'd been unable to see before.

Hope in the midst of pain.

Suddenly, the sweet smell of oranges ripening on the trees invaded her senses. And for the first time, it didn't remind her of all the bitterness she'd experienced. It was different now. *She* was different. Gabriella inhaled deeply and came to understand.

The sweetness pointed to life and how it could be if only she would surrender to it. It was the fragrance of surrender. And although it had permeated the air around her for so long, only now could she recognize it.

Surrender.

Because life may not always go the way we expect it to, but there's hope.

With God, there's always hope.

Chapter 19

Gabriella closed the Bible. "Do you think we'll ever figure it out?" Mona nodded. "I'm sure we will, but I don't think it's supposed to be easy," she said. "We'll come to understand it in time."

Gabriella sighed. "I don't why I'm in such a hurry to understand everything. I mean, look how long it took me to get to this point." She laughed and looked at her watch. "I wonder what's taking Preacher so long?"

"I'm sure he and the police chief have a lot to talk about. Imagine after all these years what it will take to sort this mess out. It will be good learn what happened to all those men, won't it?"

Gabriella nodded in agreement. "I just wish he'd hurry."

They heard a knock on the door and rushed to it to find a subdued Preacher standing on the front porch. He nodded a greeting to them. "We'd better pay Rosa and Juan Jose a visit," he said. "There's news about Rodolfo, and I'd hate for them to hear it from strangers." He started walking toward the truck and then turned around. "Let's take Samuèl with us. Juan Jose is going to need his friend."

The women followed Preacher to his truck in silence as Sammy peppered him with questions about their next preaching trip. When they got in the car, Preacher turned to Sammy. "Son, we're going to have to tell Juan Jose some sad things about his dad," he said. "He's going to need you to be strong for him."

"His dad isn't dead, is he?" he asked in a small voice.

184

"I'm afraid so."

Sammy blinked away the tears and looked out the window. He didn't speak for the rest of the ride.

When Rosa opened the door to find the group standing on her porch, she was taken back. "What's this?" she asked in Spanish. "Is everything okay?" She squinted her eyes. "Has Juan Jose done something?"

"No, senora," said Preacher. "But we have some news to give you. It's about Rodolfo." He turned to Sammy. "Will you go and find Juan Jose? Don't tell him anything yet and try to keep him out of here until we're finished talking, okay?"

Rosa smiled and waved to Sammy as he walked outside to find his friend. "Has Rodolfo been found? Is he coming home?"

Preacher took her hands and led her to the sofa. "No, I'm afraid not." He caught her up to date on everything, including the arrests of Hector, Herlinda, and one other man, and then told her about his trip to the station to learn about the fate of the men. "There are three men and Herlinda who are still alive from the group that sent the men to the U.S. There was Hector, the old police chief, and the man who ran the taxing authority here. They all denied Herlinda's accusations at first—until they were offered a deal. The tax man broke first and told what happened in exchange for a slightly reduced sentence.

"It turns out the men went to the U.S. just as the Immigration reform was happening, and many illegals were given amnesty. That was disastrous to the plans of the group because if the men were able to legally work and send back money, they would be able to repay the loans, and the group would never be able to take control of the properties. So, they changed tactics, and instead paid the coyotes to kill the men."

Rosa gasped. "My Rodolfo? The coyotes killed him, too? But he left so many years later."

Preacher nodded. "Apparently, they continued to follow the same plan all these years. It was the only way to ensure the men were never able to return and pay off the loans."

Tears flowed freely down Rosa's face, and Mona moved to sit next to her. She wrapped her arms around the woman and allowed her to cry for as long as she needed to. Finally, Rosa pulled way. "Oh, Juan Jose," she moaned. "How will I tell him this news about his father?"

Preacher stood. "With your permission, I'd like to do that. I believe it's important to treat him like a man while breaking the news to him. It will make it easier for him in the days to come."

Rosa thought for a moment and nodded. After Preacher walked outside to find the boys, Gabriella moved to sit on the other side of her.

"I'm so sorry," she said, speaking hesitantly. "I know something that may give you some comfort. Rosa, what do you know about God?"

She shook her head. "Not much. But maybe Rodolfo did. Soon after he left for the U.S., I received an envelope from him that contained only a small cross. I never understood it because he was not a religious man."

"He may have discovered something important before he died. Something he didn't have time to tell you about before..." Gabriella looked to Mona in desperation.

"Let me tell you the meaning of that cross," Mona said.

Rosa listened intently, and when Mona finished speaking, she asked, "Do you believe this? That God died for us? For me?"

"Yes. My Raul tried to tell me these things before he died. And now that I believe, I'm certain we'll see each other in Heaven."

Rosa looked at Gabriella. "Juan Jose has been talking to me about this God, but I thought it was just more of his nonsense. Do you really think Rodolfo learned of this before he died?"

Gabriella shrugged. "I don't think we can know for sure, but why else would Rodolfo mail you a cross? I think it was his way of making sure you also knew the truth."

Rosa nodded. "And Juan Jose? He is a believer too?"

The women nodded. "Okay," she said, wiping away more tears. "Tell me what I must do."

After the women led Rosa in prayer, they sat on the sofa and watched a tragic scene play out on the front porch. Preacher spoke softly to Juan Jose as they sat together on a bench while Sammy nervously hovered.

The women watched the boy's shoulders slump when Preacher finished speaking, and the stout man gently wrapped his arms around the boy. Sammy tried to hide his tears. He had obviously taken Preachers words to heart and was trying to be strong for his friend.

The women watched out the window as Juan Jose looked desperately toward Sammy, and then saw the young boy put aside his own pain and bend down to hug him. Juan Jose's lips quivered violently—the women could see it from the sofa—but he tried to put on a brave front. He nodded resolutely as Preacher spoke but kept glancing toward the house. He was worried about his mother, they knew, and Rosa couldn't sit there any longer without offering him some comfort.

"I need to go to him."

Gabriella and Mona nodded, stood and held out their hands in a gesture of support. They walked outside together to mourn with Juan Jose and tell him about the cross. They needed to give him hope that his father was safely tucked away in Heaven.

Epilogue

A few days later, Gabriella approached the cliff, reluctant to get too close. The wind whipped at her skirt and blew her dark hair across her eyes. She looked out at the sea and its waves, rolling smoothly, one after another, according to some unknowable pattern, some predestined order.

She breathed in deeply and fell to her knees. She raised her hands to the sky, no longer in fists, but open, palms facing upward.

"I'm yours," she whispered into the wind. "Please be gentle with me." She let out a sob and released it all into the hands of her King.

And her eyes shone with the light of the world.

About the Author

APRIL GEREMIA has made her living as a professional writer for 20 years, and has recently turned her attention toward her true love—fiction. She loves God, her family and friends, the sea, mysteries, and stories of people battling impossible situations. The books in this series, Souls of the Sea, have all those elements in common.

When she's not writing, you'll find her coaxing vegetables out of the ground, playing with her chickens, or whipping up a simple gourmet meal in her tiny house by the sea. Her favorite part of any day is connecting with her readers. You can find her at:

Website:
www.aprilgeremia.com

Facebook:
www.facebook.com/april.geremia

Twitter:
@april_geremia

The Next Book in the Series

The Leap of Forgiveness
Souls of the Sea: Book2

This book intertwines two love stories and a mystery that, once solved, has the potential to alter the lives of everyone involved.

What if everything you've ever been told is a lie?

When Joshua was just a young boy in the 60's, he was told his mother took her own life and left him to be raised by an emotionally absent man and a woman who had slipped into insanity because of the death of her own child. Those circumstances affected every aspect of Joshua's life but it wasn't until he met Isabelle, the red-haired bookstore owner on Bell Island, that he realized just how emotionally stifled he was. He loved her, but his tragic past kept him from fully committing. And Isabelle was tired of waiting.

Then lavender scented letters began arriving in Joshua's mailbox. The letters were signed "Mama," and they filled in the missing pieces of his early life with his mother, including why her own turbulent love story caused her to walk into the ocean one day in her best suit. They also contained God-inspired wisdom that had the potential to set Joshua on another path.

But Joshua must determine whether the letters are truly from his mother, who he believes has been dead for 20 years, or if there is an even deeper mystery that will finally explain the heartbreaking events of so long ago.

If you love inspirational books that make you feel, buy *The Leap of Forgiveness* and begin reading it today.

Watch for Book 3 in this Series: The Irrationality of Poetry - Available for pre-order August 18, 2016

TURN THE PAGE FOR A FREE PREVIEW!

The Leap of Forgiveness

Souls of the Sea: Book 2

Prologue

The letter began is soundless free fall into the future. There was no indication, no sign or subtle hint of its destiny as it twirled the through salty, humid air. The ancient lavender parchment envelope, which held the hope for one man's life and the last words of a woman, spiraled downward, until it landed on the soft cloud of waiting letters. The flowing curves of the decades old script stood out among the sterilely typed words of the present. Although the lavender scent had begun to fade, the air around the letter instantly became smoother, cleaner. The magic of the letter was such that if someone were to stop outside the mailbox and listen closely, they might hear the tides of tomorrow whispering in their ears.

Chapter One

Bell Island lay suspended in the vast body of water, having not enough. Lacking. Wanting. Although the island was surrounded by the blue-green sea, the worst drought in its history was upon it. The sea grass had burned and withered into brownish clumps, and people walked about with matted hair and deep wet circles under their arms. There was no relief; even showing had been limited to three times a week because of the water rationing. The island was being baked dry, and piece by piece, its colorful history and promising future was being chipped off and discarded into the swirling gray sea.

The relentless sun beat down on Joshua McKeon's bare back as he deftly hoisted the frayed fishing net over the boat's edge. He wiped the sweat from his brow and leaned over the net to consider his catch. Disappointed by the scaly, paltry group of fish, he picked them from the net and dropped them into the stained plastic bucket filled with seawater. Joshua looked toward the glaring sun and decided there wasn't enough time for another try. Not if he was going to make his date with Isabelle.

He grinned at the thought of her wild, red hair, pale face and patches of freckles she considered a curse, and he longed, as he did so often now, for things to be like they were when they first met. A year ago, he would have walked into her bookstore and found her immersed in one of the hundreds, perhaps thousands of books on the shelves, and she wouldn't have known he was there until he wrapped his fish-stained arms around her. She would have reacted instantly, jumping up, almost knocking over her chair and throwing herself into him, becoming an extension of him at once. Her face would have been open, full of the joy she seemed to gather and dispense each day. But day after day, month after month, just as he'd been about to let go and revel in her love, it would happen again. Just as it always did.

He'd pull back, just a little, but enough for her to notice, and she would slowly stiffen her arms and begin asking about his day. He would apologize with his eyes and then reach for her. She allowed herself to be held, but the air of unrestraint, of unconditional everything would have already floated out the window and evaporated with the sun's heat over the thick blue sea.

Joshua hadn't been ready to fall in love, but when he heard about the new bookstore in the middle of town and the fiery redhead who ran it, he'd been intrigued. Bell Island is a fishing town, and doesn't attract the grocery or fast food chains the larger towns do, so a new business is a novelty, and visiting it a major event.

That Saturday morning a little more than a year ago, when Joshua pushed open the wooden door and heard the soft jingle of the door chime, he unknowingly entered another world. One with uncharted feelings, conflict and pain and the possibility of real love and happiness.

It was a world that his life thus far had ill-prepared him for.

He'd seen her at once, partially hidden by the long wooden counter that held the cash register, fancy coffee machines and a glass case half-full of freshly baked goods. The scent of coffee, cinnamon and musty old books swirled about his head.

She'd sensed him, too, and stopped in the middle of a transaction. He brilliant blue-green eyes flitting around the room until finally landing on him like a bird settling into its nest. Joshua hadn't moved, stayed still even as she drew herself away and concentrated once again on the customer in front of her. Only when she'd counted the change and thanked the woman who purchased the books did she allow her eyes to search him out once more.

"Looking for anything in particular?" she asked. "No, wait." She stepped from behind the counter, exposing a loose white cotton skirt and snug green T-shirt. "Let me guess." She closed her eyes and put her chin in her hands. After a few moments of silence, her eyes sprang to life. "I've got it. You're an Emerson. I have a book of his essays in pretty good condition. Want to follow me?"

Joshua watched the red curls disappear behind a tall shelf of books. His first instinct was to tell her he had never read Emerson, wasn't in fact, even sure who he was. He laughed to himself as he thought of the stack of fishing books beside his bed, the only books he owned. But he didn't tell her. Instead, he followed her and wondered at the sweat forming on the palms of his hands.

It was there, in the midst of the classics that lined the old, sagging shelves he'd fallen in love. He watched her bend and push books aside, mumbling, not really caring whether he responded, searching for the book she was so sure he'd come for. It was the look of shy excitement when she found the book and handed it to him like a trophy that cinched it. In her face, he saw an openness that, up until that moment, he hadn't thought existed.

Up close, he saw that she was younger than he first thought, less than his twenty-five. There were no faint traces of lines spreading around her eyes or mouth, but when she smiled, tiny lines touched the bridge of her nose, which she'd probably crinkled as a child.

Joshua flipped through the small, brown ragged book. "I'll take it."

He silently followed her to the front of the store and ordered a cup of coffee just to prolong the transaction. He watched her hands move. Her nails were cut short, and her fingers flew over the equipment with a practiced ease, until at last, she handed him the steaming cup.

He made small talk about whether or not she liked the island and about her business, but another customer demanded her attention so he'd slipped out of the store, carrying Isabelle in his mind.

Joshua staying up all night swimming through the unfamiliar words, and by morning, he'd read the entire book. He even managed to memorize a few passages. He strolled into the bookstore the next day with the intention of asking her out, but she'd misunderstood his presence to mean he wanted another book. He left that day with a Hemingway, and not Isabelle, and then as the week went on, Faulkner, O'Connor, and Thoreau.

At the end of the week, he stood before the register, red eyed and weary from staying up every night reading, and handed her a twenty to pay for a Scott. She held on to his bag instead of giving it to him with his change. "World's fastest reader, huh?" she asked with a glint of mischief in her eyes.

"Nothing like a good book," he said, reaching for his bag.

"You know," she said, pulling it just out of his reach. "You're going to go broke if you don't ask me out soon."

Joshua stood frozen, caught. His mouth broke into a smile, then a laugh, and soon everyone in the store was looking his way. "You caught me," he said, holding up his hands in surrender.

And so it had begun.

Their first date took place on a sticky, breezy day among carnival vendors and a Ferris wheel that stretched high into the cloudless sky. The seaside fair had been Isabelle's idea. Joshua would have preferred something a little more predictable like dinner at the island's only nice restaurant. And when she first suggested it, he'd been a little disappointed by her choice. But he soon realized, and in time grew to expect, that any time with Isabelle was an event—an all-out celebration of life.

As soon as they walked through the chain linked fence that surrounded the fair, Isabelle shielded her eyes from the sun and set her sights on the enormous Ferris wheel. "Let's ride that first," she said, tugging him in that direction.

"We could," he said. "Or we could save it for last."

"Why would we want to do that?"

"Because it's the best thing here, and if we ride it first we won't have anything to look forward to."

She looked at him oddly. "Are you always that much of a pessimist?"

"Pessimist? I've always thought of it as saving the best for last."

"I don't know." She shrugged. "It seems to me you would have a lot of regrets living life that way.

The looked at each other and laughed, not letting the significance of their differences sink in, the way new couples do when they discover inconvenient incompatibilities.

As the day wore on, filled with rides and games and a laughter the came from a place deep inside, Joshua saw in Isabelle what he knew to be missing in himself. She had a thirst for life, a sense of purpose so well defined it would be impossible for someone who possesses it to ever be steered off course.

They did ride the Ferris wheel, over and over again, and each time they swooped down the circled path, they marveled at how the sea looked close enough to touch. At the end of their fifth ride, their fingers were interlocked, and their hearts were calling for them to continue the journey.

The stayed until the stars dusted the night sky and there were only a few scattered people milling around the empty grounds.

"I'm not ready to leave you," she whispered as he threw the last game ball of the evening. "Let me take you someplace."

He readily agreed, drunk with unfamiliar emotions he didn't quite know how to handle. He was there—in the moment—and for the first time in many years, he wasn't weighed down with the uncertainties of his brutal past.

They walked through town and toward the large public beach that sat just below the boardwalk. One of the hotels had a private pier that was reserved for their guests, but Isabelle ducked under the sign that declared it private, and waved him in. Joshua looked around uneasily and then followed her. They walked along the boardwalk as the night water rushed under them causing the pier to sway. Finally, they reached a white weathered cabana. It was small with wooden benches lining all but one side. Isabelle moved toward the front of the small structure, leaned over and closed her eyes.

Joshua stood mesmerized, watched her drink in the smells, the sounds of the surf. She was beautiful standing there as the wind blew her pale yellow gauze shirt against her body. She looked like she was in full control of her life, and he doubted she had ever known fear, even hesitation. He wondered what she would say if she knew how terribly afraid he felt most days, how fearful he was even in that very moment.

She opened her eyes and held out her hand. When he took it, she drew him near. "Can't you feel the life in this place," she asked softly. "I come here every day after I close the bookstore."

"And do what?"

"Read. And think."

Joshua looked out at the sea, felt for a moment—a tiny fraction of a second—the joy, the magic of the life she spoke of, but then he lost it, like the fleeting glimpse of someone you long for.

"What do you think about?"

"Everything." She smiled. "And sometimes, nothing at all."

He nodded, pretending to understand, utterly charmed by this quirky, free spirited woman. "It's nice here." And he meant it. It was the best moment he'd had in years.

The next morning, Joshua had awoken with a new sensation deep inside his abdomen that he couldn't define. He only knew one thing: he had to see Isabelle again.

Soon.

So he'd gone out to sea that day, hoisting his nets high in the shimmering sun, but never letting the boat get so far out that he couldn't see the while cabana at the end of the pier. He felt dazed, reckless, and although he sensed his fears still lurked inside him, he couldn't feel them at the moment. He thought about nothing except Isabelle and how she had already affected his life. He hadn't kissed her the night before, and he regretted it, knew he couldn't stop thinking about it until he did.

Before any of the other boats did, Joshua pulled in his nets and haphazardly collected his catch. He sailed for the docks, a man with nothing on his mind except the kiss of a woman who, only the night before, had captured his heart.

After he got home and cleaned up, he drove his rusted truck to the town deli and bought some sandwiches and fruit. Larry, the owner and a longtime friend, looked at him curiously. But Joshua was so wrapped up in his plans for the night, he didn't even notice.

Moments later, Joshua pulled up to the boardwalk and turned off his engine. He could just make out her red curls flowing into the wind, feel her presence drawing him to her like the sun pulls a flower from the ground. She looked beautiful as she sat in the cabana in the setting sun. He got out, ducked under the chain and walked toward her. She didn't see him until he was there, in the cabana, and her instant smile, her dancing eyes, told him all he needed to know.

She felt it, too.

As he sat, she held his gaze, quietly, gently, and then touched his face. She hesitantly drew him near, then stopped, unsure. When he sensed her reluctance, he gently kissed the woman he was sure had been put on the earth just for him.

Then shyly, but with a new boldness in the air, they settled into each other and ate. The talked about their lives up until that point, and Isabelle told Joshua about her courageous father and how she'd learned about life while watching him die of cancer.

"The disease stole his dreams."

"I'm sorry," he said. "Was it recent?"

"No. I was young, twelve, but old enough to understand the meaning."

He looked at her, obviously perplexed.

She took a deep breath. "My father, up until he got the news that he was ill, always did what was expected of him instead of what he truly wanted to do." She looked at Joshua and could see that he was still confused. "He worked as a manager in a printing press, but every day when he backed out of the driveway to head towards work, it was another day he wasn't doing what he truly loved."

"What was that?"

"He wanted to write a novel. I used to feel sorry for him because all he ever talked about was the story he had in his head, and how sure he was that if he just find the time to write it, the world would listen. I used to take an odd pride in the fact that he was frustrated novelist because it somehow made him unlike any of my friend's fathers. But it never occurred to me at that early age that simply talking about a dream, instead of working towards it, is just talk. The truth is, I finally came to realize he just didn't have the courage to begin his book. Until he got sick."

Joshua put his hand on her knee. "I'm sorry. What happened then?"

She shrugged, as if the memory had faded and no longer caused her pain, but Joshua saw the ache behind her courage. "He was diagnosed with lung cancer. Initially, he was given six months to live, and after he got over the anger and sadness that comes with knowing you're about to die, he got serious about his book. He began to write with a vengeance. It was as if he were trying to fit a lifetime of words into six months. I watched him go from a man who was just willing to accept whatever life handed him, good or bad, to one filled with passion and purpose." She shrugged. "The only problem was, he was dying."

"That's must have been difficult to watch."

She nodded. "I used to pretend he wasn't sick, and I imagined he'd always been that determined and strong." She squeezed Joshua's hand. "He never did finish his book. The cancer spread more quickly than anyone imagined it would, but he lived long enough for me to learn what he desperately tried to teach me in his last months. That we should squeeze the most we can out of life every single day."

She turned to look out at the sea. "It was too late for him, but I swore I wouldn't let his death be in vain. I promised him before he died that I would always live my life boldly."

"He sounds like an amazing man."

Isabelle nodded. "He was, in the end. And you? What kind of people raised a guy like you?"

He smiled mournfully. "They were not as courageous as your father, I'm afraid."

He took a breath, about to tell her of his tragic past when a group of rambunctious kids came trampling down the pier. They quickly invaded the cabana with their laughter, and by the time Joshua and Isabelle walked back to the boardwalk, the moment had passed. His story would have to wait.

The boat swayed abruptly, and now Joshua felt the dry, stagnant air force itself into his lungs as he loaded the buckets filled with fish into the cabin. That had been a little over a year ago, and Isabelle was growing impatient. When they first started dating, she had been to him like a lighthouse on a dark, thick night. She'd beckoned to him, pulled him in closer and closer until one day her realized in a panic that their lives had become intertwined. They needed each other just to survive.

He hadn't realized how quickly they grown close because he'd been too consumed with the newness of their love to notice. So on the day their world came into focus, he panicked. He'd only been truly close to one other person in his life, and since then, he'd experienced nothing but pain. And so the sense of warmth and security he always felt with Isabelle shot out of his body and flew into the cold night air.

Since then, she'd been alluding to, urging him to see the happily ever after, but it scared him, so he began to pull away. It was obvious that Isabelle was confused and frustrated by his behavior. She said she loved him, but the kind of love she desired would flow freely toward her, not run in the opposite direction.

So the distance between them continued to grow, with each one retreating further and further in their own protective spaces. Joshua wanted to follow Isabelle to the life she imagined, but something else controlled his thoughts and movements, and that something was his past, his story, and the fear of loss that had been etched into his soul at the tender age of five. So no matter how hard he tried, no matter how many times he promised her he would change, he couldn't let himself slip that last, short distance freely into the waiting arms of his love.

He knew the subject would surface at dinner, and that caused him to panic. What would he say this time? And how much longer would she wait?

Dear Reader,

I hope you enjoyed reading the first chapter of my new book. It's available at Amazon and everywhere else. I'm so excited to bring it to you! In it, Joshua uncovers a secret about his past that makes him realize everything he's believed his entire life is a lie. And as he struggles to make sense of the words in the mysterious letters he receives from his deceased mother, his world is entirely shaken.

Will Isabelle wait for him to figure it out? And how does God play into all of this?

If you want to stay current on my new releases, contests, cover reveals, giveaways and the occasional blog post, be sure to sign up for my mailing list at aprilgeremia.com.

Also, I love to hear from my readers! Please send me an email via my website and tell me what you think about my books, want you like to read about, or let me know if you need prayer.

And please, if you enjoyed the book, please consider leaving a review for it on Amazon. It really helps other readers decide whether they want to read it.

And be sure to stay tuned: *The Irrationality of Poetry*, the third book in this series, is coming in August. I'll definitely be asking for reader input on this cover!

April

Made in the USA
San Bernardino, CA
16 February 2018